THE HIGHLANDER'S NORSE BRIDE

The Hardy Heroines series (book #4)

By Cathy & DD MacRae

PRINT EDITION

PUBLISHED BY
Short Dog Press

www.cathymacraeauthor.com

License Notes

DEDICATION

*To all who
need a safe harbor*

THE HIGHLANDER'S NORSE BRIDE

Caught between two kings vying for sovereignty of the Isles and Western Scotland, Hanna of Hällstein has lost everything—and vows to repay the Scots for the deaths of her husband and children. Fleeing the smoldering ruins of her village, Hanna crosses the Strait of Mull and chooses the Laird of Clan MacLean as the object of her revenge.

Alex MacLean has buried a wife and three children. Ignoring the clamors for him to wed again and produce an heir, he finds himself drawn to a Norse refugee who defies him and tests the limits of his patience—and his power as Laird.

Torn between revenge and honor, Hanna fears setting aside her vow of vengeance means she has lost her reason for living. Alex is determined to save her, even if it means defying the king.

The Highlander's Norse Bride

*In the 13th century, the king of Scotland had little control in the
Western Highlands and in the isles to the north and west. A rich
culture of Gaelic and Norn existed here, and power lay in the hands
of the chiefs. Much of Western Scotland and the Isles gave their
allegiance to the king of Norway.*

*In 1249, King Alexander II prepared to invade the Hebrides and
Western Scotland. After 5 years of failed negotiations with Norway
to purchase these areas, King Alexander broke his association with
King Haakon and set out to take the Isles and Western territories by
force.*

*In the years to come, two kings would perish during this battle for
sovereignty—along with many people given the choice to change
their alliance to the Scottish king . . .*

Or die.

Chapter One

MacLean Castle, 1248

Arbela gently wrapped her arms about her brother's shoulders, wincing at the ridge of collar bone evident beneath her hands. Wings of silver graced his temples, glittering in his night-dark hair, evidence of the passage of time. Though, as his twin, Arbela's own dark locks glistened with a like reminder.

"Will ye not come inside?" she murmured in his ear.

Alex patted her hand. "I am only remembering, lass, not fashin'."

She smiled. "Ye sound more like father every day."

"I had no idea when he brought us here from the Holy Land almost thirty years ago, I would have so much of what I hold dear planted in this rocky soil."

"We each began new lives here," Arbela replied. "Do ye ever miss the desert?"

"Sometimes. I miss our youth, our freedom. What of ye?"

Arbela gave a soft laugh. "'Tis my home, now, though I do miss the desert heat from time to time. I find the wind and snow rather bracing, but I could do with a bit less rain."

She kneaded his shoulders, smoothing the taut muscles, giving him what comfort she could. Together they stared out over the small graveyard, the fresh-turned soil a scar against the rippling grass that would fade with time. Two carved wooden crosses flanked Annag's grave. One for the twins, born too early to survive, the for eight-year-old Donal, named for his grandsire and taken from them the same winter as the elder of a fever.

Alex shook his head as if to chase away the memories that even now tore at Arbela's heart.

"I thank ye for not scolding me for my thoughts this day, Sister. I know I should be caring for wee Gillian who misses her ma. I should grieve my wife, not sit here thinking on other things." He paused and Arbela gave him time to gather his words. "I do grieve her death—but 'tis a ghostly pain, not the wrenching—" His voice broke and Arbela hugged him tighter, knowing what tore at his heart this day, understanding too well the grief of a lost child.

"It does not become easier, does it?" she asked, her heart breaking for her beloved brother. Each had experienced heartache over the years, but such loss seemed to touch him more than most.

He shook his head, beyond words. Arbela winnowed her fingers through his hair as though he were a lad. "Father would be so proud of ye," she said. "All ye have accomplished with the shipping trade. Expanding our borders, though it required dealing with the King of the Isles—tip-toeing betwixt the Norse and Scottish kings. Bringing peace to our northern border."

"Ye did not care for that business, did ye?" Alex asked, his voice soft, laced with faint humor.

Latching onto any memory that lightened Alex's heart, Arbela plunged into the early days after their arrival in Scotland. "I was understandably upset to learn my dear brother proposed an alliance with the MacGillonays," she replied wryly.

"What better time?" he asked, though the argument was an old one. "Auld man MacGillonay and his viperous sons were dead— thanks to ye—and the succession was in turmoil. My marriage to Annag brought her family—a distant relation to the auld laird—into prominence, and later, to the lairdship. Better them than the toadies vying for the position."

"'Tis true. But 'twas a bit much to swallow so soon after

Bram's kidnapping and their attempt to take over Dunfaileas."
Arbela suppressed a small shudder at the memory. Her five-year-old
stepson, now grown to manhood and as braw and fearless as any
man, had faced down his captors—at her prompting—spoiling Laird
MacGillonay's son's last attempt to wreak revenge on the MacKerns
for the deaths of his father and younger brother.

"We have all thrived with your care and wisdom, Alex. Your
years as chief of Clan MacLean have been good ones. And ye have
more to look forward to, watching Gillian grow."

He stiffened beneath her arms, and she cursed silently. His
years had been punctuated by the births of four children—and the
deaths of three. And now his wife.

He inhaled deeply, then released his breath. He glanced over his
shoulder and gave her a sad smile. "I grow old, I fear," he said. "The
years pile together, leaving my regrets brilliantly clear, whilst
muting those things I did not care so much about."

"Ye are but forty-five summers, brother. But I understand,"
Arbela replied. "And I am here with ye as long as ye need."

"What about your husband's needs?" he queried, a subtle return
to humor marking his voice. "I seem to recall a hulking man who
does not care to have ye long from his side."

"He is well, and will have our granddaughters at Dunfaileas to
distract him for the next few days." Arbela chuckled. "'Twill make
him all the happier to see me when I return home."

"Life has been kind to ye, I believe," Alex noted. "Ye grew to
love the man ye married, and you have two bonny daughters, a son
and a step-son who dote on ye and coddle ye in your old age."

Arbela slapped his shoulder lightly. "My old age?" she asked,
her voice sliding upward in mock outrage. "I will thank ye to keep
your thoughts behind your teeth." She leaned her cheek into his
shoulder to take away the sting of her words. It was clear Alex felt

their years this day. Burying his wife of nearly thirty years, no matter the scant fondness between them—unlike the passionate love Arbela had found with her husband—created a hole in his life. Arbela wondered how he would choose to fill the void, and if one small child would be enough.

"Ye will remarry," she asserted. "In time, ye will find a woman who appreciates ye."

Alex's head swayed heavily. "I could have loved her," he said, gaze once again on the fresh-turned earth over his wife's grave.

Arbela stroked his arm. "Ye cared for her," she comforted. "Annag was content."

"But I dinnae love her as she deserved, Bela. My wife never knew what it was to be truly loved."

"And, my brother, neither did ye."

Chapter Two

May, 1249, 1 year later
Village of Hällstein, Isle of Mull

The rumble of barking dogs roused Hanna from sleep at the same instant her husband rolled from their bed. Steel rasped on leather as he slid his sword from its sheath, the pad of bare feet on the wood floor surprisingly light for a man of his bulk. Torvald did not waste time telling her to stay safely behind. Women in her world fought to defend what was theirs. She would attend her duties as head of the women of the clan.

Hanna slipped from the bed, shoving her feet into thin leather boots, arms into a kirtle stained dark that would blend with the shadows. Placing three small daggers into hidden sheaths, she followed Torvald into the dark hall and down the stairway. They separated in the hall, silent as ghosts, though movement in the longhouse rustled as others gathered to the alarm. Shouts in the yard rose, torches flared, and children were herded into the safe room beneath the floor of the hall.

"Stay silent," she warned, laying a gentle hand on her daughter's shoulder as she mounted the ladder to the underground passage. Twelve-year-old Signy paused, sending Hanna an anguished look. "Ye are a good daughter," Hanna said past a lump in her throat. The commotion rose to a fever pitch outside the protective walls, and both she and Signy knew this was no simple raid. "Go," Hanna told her. "Be safe."

Signy nodded, squaring her shoulders as she met Hanna's eyes one last time. A moment later, her head disappeared into the shadows.

"I will not go with the children," her son stated. "I will help defend the village."

Hanna stared at Sten's ten-year-old form, gangly and tall, with only a hint of his father's bulk. He was still a child, seeking her permission rather than his father's, small axe clasped tight in his fist, a dagger at his belt.

"I cannot have ye amongst the men," she said. "They fight as one, and ye have not yet the training. Find two others such as ye and defend the door."

Sten nodded and glanced at the group behind him, motioning to a pair of his closest friends. Hanna gave them one last look as she prayed they would come to no harm. She had done what she could.

Stepping through the door into the yard, Hanna joined several other women, their faces grim in the torchlight. Beyond the edge of the yard, men armed and girded with steel struggled ashore from boats that pitched in the tide. The men of Hällstein pressed them back, the clang of metal harsh in the fire-pierced darkness.

Cries of wounded men reached the women, and two from amongst them followed the sounds, their job to tend the injured. Around Hanna, women fell to their tasks, no words necessary, and none arising from throats dry with dread.

Another ship loomed against the shore, bow and planks aglow, reflecting the dance of Torvald's bonfires as the flames leapt high on the rocky beach, illuminating the battle in vivid red and gold. Hanna's heart stuttered at the sight of bodies amidst the boulders. Men from the ships bounded over the seething mass of dying men, swords glinting, headed for the longhouse.

Time faded, became as nothing, the action around her slowing to an unbearable crawl. Her ears picked out Torvald's shouts from amid the other voices as the fighting heightened. Hanna strode forward, skirts tucked inside her belt to free her movements, shaking her arms to loosen her muscles. A man she did not recognize slipped from the fight, his attention on the empty yard before the longhouse. His gaze swept over Hanna, dismissing her as a threat—the last mistake he would make that night. Hanna stepped sideways, into his guard, causing him to pull up short in surprise. Without hesitation, she drove her dagger into his belly just beneath his breastbone, angling upward into the thick muscle between his chest and abdomen.

His gasp of surprise turned to one of distress as he fought to drag air into his lungs. Not lingering to watch him die, Hanna met the next enemy.

* * *

Exhaustion dulled Hanna's senses, deadened the pain of injury and loss. The few women crowding around her appeared as indifferent as she felt, shoulders drooped, clothing torn and bloodied. Yet defiance glinted their eyes as the dawning sun illuminated the charred remains of the village and the longhouse. Hanna leaned to one side, retching as bile rose, reeling from her imaginings of what lay beneath the burned timbers.

Straightening, her gaze darted from one guard to the next, seeking answers. Had the women and children hidden in the secret passage escaped? Had they been trapped? Overcome by smoke? Had soldiers entered before they torched the structure, taking prisoners? Or leaving no survivors? What had been Signy and Sten's fate? Were these few women around her all who remained of their clan?

Perhaps a lucky few had scrambled to safety amid the confusion as the wooden structure was torched, but it was clear none lived. Her gaze drifted over the bloodstained ground between the yard and the shore where her husband and his men had fought their final battle.

She would remember this for the rest of her days, but for now she clung to the next breath, the next moment, pushing aside the terrible emptiness within.

She pressed a hand against the ripped sleeve of her kirtle. In the moments it had taken her to stem the bleeding of the jagged knife wound, she had been captured and brought to the circle of detained women. Her fingers met with clotted blood, the fabric soaked through. The agony had settled to a dull throb, though she knew the pain would soon return. She fought through the dizziness of blood loss, determined to remain standing and hear her fate.

Men draped in checkered woolen cloth marking them as Scots swaggered around the group of women, leering at them, their bearded, blood-spattered faces a horrific sight in the dim light. A few traipsed across the yard, loading the ships with what loot they'd discovered before setting the hall ablaze. Hällstein's riches had been in the sea, not measured in gold or precious gems, though a few treasures passed from generation to generation had graced the hall's tables and coffer.

"What do ye want?" Hanna demanded, the sight of the utter ruin about her prodding her anger and despair. Sending their leader, a man marked by his air of command and detachment from the activity around him, a look of defiance and scorn, she labeled herself the spokesperson for the remaining villagers.

He returned her gaze, one brow arched. After a moment's hesitation, he stepped closer. Halting a few feet away, feet braced a shoulder's width apart, balanced slightly forward, he raked her with a derisive glare.

"Our sovereign king, Alexander of Scotland, bids welcome to his newest subjects," he mocked.

"We are subject to no king of Scotland," Hanna spat. "Indeed, if these are the actions of your king, he is despicable and deserves no man's loyalty."

"My king bade us take back the isles," the man replied. "By force or by transfer of allegiance—whichever is most successful."

Hanna's brows rose. "I heard no offer of clemency by aligning myself with the Scottish king," she noted. She tossed her gaze about the scattered bodies of her clansmen. "I doubt they were presented with the suggestion, either."

The Scot shrugged. "I was not told which to offer. And I doubt the king cares so long as I bring him the land."

"And what of the items ye have loaded onto your ship?" Hanna asked. "Will ye bring him what little gold we had?"

A smile creased the man's face, parting his lips to reveal his teeth in a predatory grin that sent a shiver down Hanna's spine. He closed the distance between them until she nearly gagged on the overwhelming odor of unwashed male and fresh blood. "Neither the gold nor the bounty I see before me will pass from my hands," he whispered. "Some things I willnae share."

A gull shrieked overhead. Hanna inhaled a smoky reminder of death. Defiance warred with anger. Anger for the lives wasted in the land struggle between two kings. Anger for the arrogance of the man before her who cared naught for the shame he would inflict on the remaining women of her village.

"Come with me," the Scot commanded. He waved a hand over the clustered group of women. "Do with them as ye wish," he called to his men. Jeers of excitement and approval rose, hands grabbed, clutching clothing and flesh. Shrieks rose as the women fought back, making up in ferocity what they lacked in strength. Hanna twisted away as the leader reached for her, stomping the side of his knee as hard as she could, gratified by his grunt of pain and surprise.

He shifted his weight to one side, lightly toeing the ground with the injured leg to maintain balance. Hanna did not give him a chance to settle, but aimed a kick for his groin. He pivoted to the side, but not fast enough. Her booted foot caught him squarely between his legs. With a thin shriek, he crumpled to the ground. With a quick, stabbing motion, Hanna shoved her blade between two vertebrae at the base of his skull, killing him instantly.

She spun about, finding herself outside the melee. One by one, the women were subdued, though the price in gouges, dislocated appendages and one man whose ability to see again was questionable, had taken its toll on their captors. Breathless and muttering uneasily, they cast infuriated looks at the still-defiant women. One woman caught Hanna's gaze.

"Run," she mouthed as her hands were jerked roughly behind her back. Hanna shook her head.

Another nodded at her. "Avenge us."

Taking her chance, Hanna ran.

Chapter Three

Alex stared at the royal missive on his desk. He'd known King Alexander since arriving in Scotland nearly twenty-seven years earlier, when the then twenty-three-year old king had married his eleven-year-old bride and Alex was a brash twenty-year-old fresh from the Holy Land. Unlike many living in Western Scotland, or on the Western Isles, Alex and his father had remained true to the Scottish king, though it cost them in war and pirating with their neighbors who swore allegiance to King Haakon of Norway—or the current King of the Isles.

For years, an active push by King Alexander to gain the Isles as part of Scotland had met with resistance from King Haakon. This time, according to the words carefully inscribed on the parchment on the desk, the king did not mean to fail.

Reaching for a map—though he knew the area the king referred to in his missive well—Alex considered King Alexander's request.

". . . gathering a fleet to purge the Western Isles of those pledged to Norway and make them subjects of Scotland. We require your assistance as your family is most prominent in ship-building, and neighbors with the MacDougall, whom the king of Norway has appointed King of the Isles . . ."

Aid in attacking the MacDougall? Alex snorted. Fondness for the king did not mean he found the man's current quest to be sane—or easy. He ran a fingertip over the parchment, drawing an imaginary line from MacLean Castle on Lochaline to the MacDougall stronghold at Dunstaffnage. The distance was not great, but the difficulties of what King Alexander proposed lay far beyond the abilities of a mere ship-builder.

"Edan!" Alex knew his captain would be nearby if not training with the soldiers. Over the past months—since his wife had died—Alex had left much of the running of the clan to Edan, choosing to spend his time aboard one of his ships. The trip to Iberia and back had taken the better part of a year, and King Alexander's missive had arrived only days after his return to Morvern. Just his luck to avoid pirates only to be caught up in the king's latest broil against Norway.

He rose from his chair and strode from his solar to the great hall. Spying Edan seated at a table alone, he crossed to the long bench.

"Read this," he said without preamble, tossing the parchment to the table and lowering his body to straddle the bench. "Tell me what ye think."

Edan wiped his mouth and fingers on a square of linen and swallowed the bite he'd just taken. "Missive from the king?" he asked, an eye on the elaborate seal at the top of the parchment. His slow grin was contagious. "And ye only home these past few days. Ye work fast, Alex MacLean. Are ye in a spot of trouble?"

"Depends on what ye call trouble. If ye mean the king's plans to besiege Dunstaffnage and end the Norse hold over the Isles and Western Scotland, then, aye. I was under the impression King Alexander was in negotiations with King Haakon for the possession of the Isles."

Edan glanced up sharply. "His Majesty has tried for the past five years to redeem the Isles and western territories from Norway, but King Haakon appears more interested in expanding his borders than selling to Scotland. King Alexander recently broke ties with Norway, and 'tis rumored he will move soon to gain the land by force. I dinnae know if he has commanded invasions of the Isles or simply turned a blind eye, but raids have picked up of late. Often with severe reprisals from those who willnae submit to Scotland's rule."

"Tell me," Alex invited. "I have been abroad."

Pushing his trencher away, Edan accepted a refill of ale before he settled to Alex's question. "King Alexander wishes a unified Scotland. And ye will recall King Haakon raided the Scottish coast not so many years ago. His man, Ewan of Argyll, of Dunstaffnage Castle, now styles himself King of the Isles and refuses to abandon his ties to Norway."

He took a long sip from his mug and placed it on the table. Hunching forward, he leaned his forearms on his knees, steepling his fingertips together. "The king is amassing both an army and an armada. Ye know his reputation against those who rebel."

His gaze met Alex's. Alex's heart thumped as he considered Edan's implications. King Alexander, for all the good he'd achieved for Scotland, was noted for his brutality when crossed.

"Dear God. He means to clear the Isles of the Norse one way or another."

"Aye. Turn their allegiance or bury them. One way or another 'twill soon be Scottish soil at this rate. We have accepted a few refugees here, though I have managed to keep it quiet."

Alex's eyebrows rose. "Accepting Norse refugees into a household sworn to the Scottish king?" He smiled to cover the pain Edan's words brought. The fate of innocents whose only crime was not being on the side of the victorious had plagued him most of his adult life. "Good. I am glad ye did. Have they assimilated into the clan?"

Edan shrugged and leaned back in his chair. "For the most part. Though if ye see a lass with Viking blonde hair tending the tables,

18

ye shouldnae remark upon it."

"I confess I have been too preoccupied with wrapping up the details of my trip to make note of the serving lasses."

"And ye've yer hands full with yer wee lass. 'Tis plain to see she enjoyed the voyage as well."

Alex laughed. "She charmed everyone from Ayr to Barcelona. Her nurse is no longer certain what language the lass speaks." He softened. "I am pleased she went. I dinnae know a wee lass could be such a companion—or a comfort—all at the bright young age of five. And now, a year later, she is quite accomplished."

"I admit I was shocked when ye announced she was to travel with ye. I'm not certain I would have taken on such a task."

"I couldnae bear to leave her so soon after her ma died," Alex admitted, lingering guilt shooting through him anew. He shifted in his seat against the unwelcome sentiment.

Edan's lifted brow indicated he noted Alex's discomfort, but he did not pursue the subject. "I am happy she lifted yer spirits." He nodded to the missive which lay on the table between them. "What will ye do with the king's request?"

Alex sighed, the weight of responsibility dropping heavily to his shoulders. "I can do naught but view it as a command. I will order the fitting of one of our merchant ships to hold soldiers, with accommodations for the king, should he care to join me, and make myself available to his whims." Alex arched a brow. "And pray for Divine deliverance."

Chapter Four

Hanna's heart thumped painfully in her chest, the sound loud in her ears, overwhelming her hearing. Nausea from the pain in her arm rose, and she swallowed hard. She stumbled to a halt and crouched in the shadow of a large boulder, breathing deeply as she strove to control the pain. Minutes passed before she was aware of the soft chirp of land birds and the occasional screech of a gull. Waves slapped against the shore below the cliff and sunlight sparkled on the water.

She'd reached the hidden entrance to the escape route from beneath the longhouse not long after daybreak, taking care to avoid being followed. But she found no one nearby, not even evidence the rock hiding the opening had been moved. Her last hope dashed, Hanna fell to the ground, her tears of anguish drenching the rocky soil beneath her.

Every muscle in her body ached as if she'd aged years. Her head throbbed with pain and despair. She rolled groggily to a sitting position and leaned against the boulder, knees drawn to her chin, fighting the urge to leave. Her heart was bound to this spot, but her head, unwilling to give up, warned her the men's hunt for her would be ruthless—and the isle would not hide her forever.

Frida's last words to her rose in her mind. *Avenge us.*

Rising stiffly from the ground, Hanna reluctantly trod the path to the cliffs, clutching her arm tight to alleviate even a fraction of the pain. She arrived a short time later at the narrow water separating the island from the Scottish mainland. The scent of smoke and char clung to her clothing, stained the inside of her nose.

But only the faintest smudge behind her on an otherwise bright sky attested to the horror she'd fled.

It was time to make a decision. She could not linger on the island.

MacLean or MacDougall? MacLean is closer. Much closer. MacDougall would provide refuge as he has ties with the king of Norway. The cries of the defeated women echoed in her head. She firmed her resolve. *MacLean is powerful, and sides with Scotland's king. I will not seek the comfort of MacDougall's hall, but rather the cold oblivion that awaits me after I avenge my family's deaths.*

She checked the rough bandage about her upper arm then rose, glancing up and down the coastline for a vessel to carry her across the strait. In fair weather, even a small boat would suffice. She could see the far coast easily and the trip wouldn't take long if she judged the current right.

They will not suspect I would flee to MacLean. Hanna glanced over her shoulder but saw no hunting party of raiders seeking her. She gathered her skirts and stepped to the edge of the cliff, drawn to a smudge of weathered gray amid the darker hues of the rocks.

A boat! Whether it would bear her across the strait or not, she'd quickly learn. And the Scottish laird would soon discover what it meant to side with a king who slaughtered innocents.

* * *

The walls of MacLean Castle rose forbiddingly from the stone above the inlet. Hanna paused, noting the open gates, the guards at the towers and upon the lofty parapet. The structure could have easily contained her longhouse—perhaps most of her village—its proportions much larger than anything she'd ever seen. For a moment, she was uncertain if she'd chosen wisely. The walls of the MacDougall stronghold were said to be solidly built and impregnable—an admirable refuge. She drew a deep breath as Frida's face hovered in her mind.

The MacDougall's alliance might be with King Haakon, but her vengeance lay with the Scots.

Smoke drifted toward her, the aroma of cooking reminding her food had not been a priority in her flight across Mull. She ignored the growl of her stomach and strode toward the village, matching her pace with the people around her, engendering little more than fleetingly curious stares as men and women hurried about their tasks. Now that she'd completed the first part of her goal, she would seek a healer and what shelter she could and begin forming a plan for revenge.

Hanna woke before the sun, stiff and aching from the uncomfortable spot she'd chosen to rest. She'd bartered her finest dagger to the healer who'd cleansed and stitched her wound without question. Bedraggled, limp with exhaustion, and in a strange place, Hanna had decided the darkest corner between two shops near the dock would be as safe as any to seek rest. She'd watched the people from her hiding place until she collapsed into a stupor—sailors who lingered at the tavern until the doors closed, serving women who dodged drunken advances, and women who welcomed the chance at a coin. Exhaustion at last overtook her and she slept, all but dead to the noises around her.

A startled cry grabbed Hanna's attention. Carefully lifting her head, she peered past the stacked barrels blocking her view. A young girl, scarcely in her teens—reminding Hanna strikingly of her daughter—cowered only a few feet away, her frightened face lit by an errant ray of sun that forced its way into the cluttered alley. From the length of the shadows, Hanna was startled to note the morning well advanced.

Men loomed on either side of the girl, the shaft of sunlight illuminating drunken leers tilting precariously on seamed, weather-beaten faces.

"Give us a sample, lass," one crooned. "I'm nae so drunk any longer."

"All the bonny ones were taken by the time we woke," another complained. "Me cock doesnae work so well after three tankards, anyway."

"Six!" boasted a third. "Mine requires six before giving up. Limp as a shank of wet cloth I was last night." He made a rude motion with one fisted hand. "But I'm ready now!"

The girl shook her head violently, causing her pale blonde hair to sparkle in the light. Hanna's heart clenched. A dagger slipped from its sheath beneath her sleeve into her hand. She tightened her fingers on the worn grip, straining to hear the next words.

"I am no *skjøge*," the girl whimpered, her attempt at bravado failing as the men pressed closer.

"But ye *are* Norse, aye?" the first one asked eagerly, lifting a hand to touch her glimmering hair. He brought a lock to his nose and inhaled deeply. "The scent of a refugee," he quipped. He grinned. "Yer men are all dead, ye have nae home. Spread yer bonny legs and let a real man show ye what ye're missing. A little wear and tear for a bit of coin is nae real hardship."

Fury slammed through Hanna. Ignoring the protest from her bandaged arm, she sprang from her hiding place, sending barrels thudding hollowly to the cobbled path. The three men glanced up, angry at the interruption. The girl drew back in horror, tears streaking her cheeks.

Images of Signy flashed before Hanna's eyes, igniting her rage at failing to save her daughter. "Let her go!"

"Be gone, auld hag," one snarled. "We have nae interest in ye."

"Release the girl and ye shall live," Hanna growled, forcing her words through jaws tight with anger.

Two of the men guffawed—the third eyed the blade in her hand.

"She has a dagger," he said, his voice low and worried.

The leader flashed a look of annoyance at the more cautious man. "She's naught but a woman," he declared. "*This* is how ye treat women!"

He grabbed the girl and yanked her against him, ripping the neckline of her gown, smothering her shriek with his mouth. In two swift steps, Hanna was behind him, her dagger plunged deep in his lower back. She jerked the blade upward, severing the large blood vessel to his kidney.

The man stiffened, his head snapped back as a cry of pain warbled from his lips. Hanna pushed the girl away, grasped the man's chin and jerked his head firm against her shoulder. With one fluid move, she dragged her blade across the taut skin of his neck, slicing deep. She held his body a moment longer as his life spilled, then let him drop to the ground. Before either of the other two men could respond, she whirled, hands spread wide in anticipation.

"Who is next?"

Chapter Five

Alex finalized the discussions with the master builder over refitting the *Porpoise* for the king's requirements. He tossed the end of his plaide over his shoulder and left his cabin, the tug to remain and take to the open seas again strong. But there would be days ahead in which the king would require his presence. His responsibility to the crown would have to come first.

Sea spray caressed his face as he crossed the ship's deck, clinging to the wool of his plaide like sparkling diamonds. Sunlight warmed the air, striping the wood beneath his feet. The walk to the castle was not far, but three soldiers fell into rank with him for protection. Together they strode to the village, responsibilities closing on Alex with every step.

A woman's shriek split the air, and Alex's hand flew to the hilt of his sword, his gaze sweeping the area around him.

"There, Laird," one of his soldiers commented, pointing to an alley between the cooper's shop and a small, disreputable tavern.

Alex strode into the passageway, his soldiers spreading out behind him, thwarting the possibility of a trap. To his shock, a woman faced him, rising out of the carnage at her feet like a wrathful Valkyrie.

Blood spattered one sleeve of her gown and trailed in a vivid slash across her skirt. Her hair straggled about her face, golden tendrils lifting about her head in the breeze. Her age was uncertain, but piercing green eyes blazed from her face. Her hands waved gently before her as if seeking their next target, a long slender blade winking dully in the dappled light. The man at her feet did not appear likely to rise again, his head tilted at an angle that bespoke death, the blood at his neck soaking liberally into the cloth of his filthy leine.

Two other men leapt to sudden action, approaching Alex with wildly waving hands, shouting each to be heard above the other. Slipping swords free, Alex and his soldiers warned them back. Dropping into silence, the men held their distance, shooting anxious glances between him and the woman who refused to alter her stance.

The heated scent of fresh blood rose to Alex's nostrils. A young lass, perhaps fourteen years of age, huddled against the tavern wall, on the verge of bolting. Terror shone from her wide eyes, one hand grasping a handful of torn cloth at the neck of her gown.

A dull throb rose in Alex's head, building with the relentlessness of a smithy's hammer as he was catapulted back in time into a memory he'd all but forgotten.

The heat of the desert sun scorched his face, beat down on his shoulders. The horse beneath him shifted uneasily, the stench of blood and char heavy in the air.

An expletive rolled from Bohemond's lips and Philip and Alex exchanged startled glances. "Damn them—and damn—" The prince broke off, obviously unable to find words to express his anger.

"We are too late," Philip sighed, his voice bitter. His hands gripped the reins tighter, his knuckles white.

Bile rose in Alex's throat as they dismounted the restless horses and strode with the prince's soldiers through the small village. Men and women sprawled lifeless in the dust, pierced with spears, cleaved with swords and axes. Blood-soaked earth clung to Alex's boots as he walked, unable to find an unsoiled space to place his feet.

A whimper pulled his attention to a nearly nude form crumpled against the remains of a charred wall. Stepping closer, he saw the body twitch, its fingers blackened with drying blood. Glazed eyes stared at him, and with a shock that nearly heaved the contents of his stomach, he realized the girl—likely no more than ten or twelve years of age from the small buds of her breasts and lack of body hair—had been brutalized. Her lips moved soundlessly and he knelt beside her, touching the side of her face gently with his fingertips. Her eyes closed and she turned her face into his soft caress as if seeking comfort. His heart broke, and he pulled the child into his arms, rocking her gently as she breathed her last sigh.

The young lass in the alley gasped and shoved her fist in her mouth against a further outburst. Through a red haze, Alex fought back to the present.

"What happened?" he demanded.

One of the men pointed to the Valkyrie. "She killed him! Bloody Norse whore killed him!"

The other nodded vigorously. "And he's a Scot! The penalty is death!"

Alex forced himself to relax the grip on his sword, forced the tension from his shoulders. He pointed the tip of his sword toward the young girl who clung to the older woman.

"What did these men do to ye?"

The girl shrank back, shaking her head.

"Ye will tell me what happened," Alex commanded, ignoring the lass' obvious discomfort. "Now."

The Valkyrie murmured something to the girl, too low for him to catch the words. The lass shook her head again.

"She is frightened," the woman said.

Alex's sword tip swung to her. "I dinnae wish to hear the tale from ye. I am waiting for this one to speak." He dismissed the woman, his patience fraying.

"My lord . . .." The girl faltered and ducked behind the woman once again.

"Speak!" Alex roared. The two miscreants shuffled their feet, more than willing to voice their accusations once again. Alex's soldiers advanced. The lass burst into tears.

"I will not tolerate this abuse of an innocent child," the Valkyrie warned, placing an arm about the lass' waist.

Astonished, Alex sent her a questioning look. "Nor do I," he growled. "But her account is crucial."

"My lord." The lass' sobs snuffled to a halt. "This one," she pointed to the man at her feet, "accosted me. I . . . I did not wish it."

"What did he do?" Alex asked, gentling his voice.

"He," she swallowed. "He grabbed me and pulled me against him." She bit her lip, anger lighting a slow flame in her eyes. "And kissed me."

"I see yer gown," Alex said. "'Twas not a kiss. 'Twas an assault." He nodded to the older woman. "And she attacked him on yer behalf." It was hardly a question, but a prod for her to finish her tale.

The girl glanced up at the Valkyrie, admiration on her face. "She warned him first."

Alex faced the dead man's friends. "Was this the way of it?"

The two men shuffled their feet, their gazes averted, unable to swear to their friend's innocence. One ventured a glare at Alex. "The woman is Norse. She has no right to kill a Scot. 'Tis our right to demand justice! Take her to the baron!"

Alex sent him a cold look. "Ye will receive justice. I am the baron."

He gestured to the miscreants. "Take them to the dungeon. I will tolerate no abuse of women or children here. Hang them on the morrow."

* * *

28

Hanna shook with cold and the realization she'd likely sealed her fate. As a Norsewoman in a village held by a Scottish lord, her action—while justified in her mind—merited death. Her heart pounded and bile rose in her throat. She was not sorry she'd killed the scum at her feet. Only that it had been necessary.

"Take them to the dungeon," Laird MacLean commanded with a sweep of his arm. To Hanna's surprise, his gesture included the two disreputable men—not herself or the girl whose life she'd saved. She snapped her gaze to the imposing man, startled by the blazing heat of the laird's scrutiny, recognizing a disgust deep within him—though whether of a Norsewoman who'd killed one of his own, or of men who preyed on innocents, she did not know.

Protests rose loudly from the two men, disbelieving that *they* appeared to be at fault, when it was clear this *Norsewoman* had killed a Scot, while they had only sought a moment of the lass's time.

The young girl slipped her cold hand in the crook of Hanna's elbow. Heedless of the bloody mess of Hanna's gown and the dead body at her feet, the girl pressed against Hanna, her body trembling. Hanna touched her cheek to the top of the girl's head, acknowledging her presence and need for comfort. Wary as a wolf ready to battle for her cub, her eyes never left the baron.

His gaze, stern and unyielding, silenced the miscreants' words and accusations. Sheathing his sword, he waited until two of his soldiers marched the men away, then turned back to Hanna.

"Are ye hurt?"

To Hanna's surprise, his voice rolled quietly over her, the biting anger softened into gentle inquiry. A tiny part of her responded to his apparent concern, but she recoiled as if slapped. He was a Scot, her enemy! He wished only to trap her. She would not trust him.

Hanna glanced about, finding no escape.

Their gazes locked, each fighting for the upper hand. Hanna refused to be cowed, fear holding her back rigid, keeping her heart pounding at an impossible rate, ready to flee. She flexed her hand, adjusting the grip on her dagger. She would not give in to the Scot.

Laird MacLean released a long, deep breath and inclined his head, handing her the victory. Hanna braced for his next move. He raised one hand and crooked a finger.

"Come with me."

Chapter Six

Frozen in place like a downed hawk caught in the gaze of a hungry wolf, the woman watched him with wary eyes. Giving her the opportunity to calm, Alex pivoted on his heel and strode a few steps away. After a moment, he heard the whisper of steel on leather as she tucked the blade away. He faced her, noting the flash of her dark green eyes, the authoritative tilt to her chin. Alex hid a smile, not certain why her defiant attitude appealed to him.

"Ye will not harm this child," she said, her hands resting firmly on the girl's slender shoulders.

"Ye are both under MacLean protection," Alex replied. "No harm will come to either of ye."

Neither woman responded, their manners guarded.

"Are ye newly arrived?" Alex asked. The two women exchanged glances. The younger nodded hesitantly.

"Ye will need a place to sleep and work to keep ye fed," Alex noted. "Help is always needed in the kitchen. Come with me and I will introduce ye to Jean." He eyed the bandage on her arm. "She will see to the tending of your wound."

Silent communication flowed between the woman and girl in the barely perceptible squeeze of the woman's blood-stained fingers on the slender shoulders and the girl's faint answering nod. Alex gestured to his remaining guard and strode from the alley as the buzz of anger slipped away, replaced with disgust.

Shite! What was King Alexander thinking, giving men free rein on conquering the Isles?

He chanced a glance over his shoulder, pleased to see the two

Norsewomen following. The lass was pale, still frightened over her encounter and the manner in which she'd been saved. Was the older woman her ma? She seemed scarcely old enough to have a daughter of that age, but he wasn't adept at guessing women's ages.

Crowds parted as he led the small entourage through the castle gates. Boots shuffled on the stone parapet above and Alex caught a glimpse of curious faces, guards alert to the laird's return. Alex summoned a lad with a jerk of his chin.

"Find Jean. Tell her I have need of her."

"Aye, Laird," the boy replied, darting across the yard to the hall.

Alex turned to the women following. "Welcome to MacLean Castle. We will rest and take refreshment in my solar."

The older woman halted, eyes widened, nostrils flared as though scenting danger.

"I have promised safety, and ye shall have it," he reassured her, understanding her wariness. "Though ye are a formidable warrior, I dinnae have to resort to subterfuge to have ye captured and thrown into the dungeon. That is neither my wish nor my intent."

"I do not trust a man loyal to Scotland's king." the woman growled, her chin tilted up in defiance.

"Trust yer own instinct," Alex replied. "My word is my bond."

With a glance to the lass at her side, the woman appeared to deliberate on his words before she at last released a short breath. "I accept on her behalf."

Alex nodded. "I will ask Jean for water and mayhap a clean gown as well for ye both."

"I do not ask for charity," the woman bristled. "Water will suffice."

"I meant no insult, nor do I offer help beyond yer immediate comfort," Alex replied, somewhat irritated by the woman's prickly manner. He stepped through the great doors and led the pair past servants who paused in their duties to stare openly. Opening the door to his solar, he ushered the women inside. He leaned out into the hall, motioning a serving lass near, and sent her to rummage suitable gowns for his guests.

A wide-eyed lad, giving the Valkyrie a wide berth, set two buckets of water near the hearth then fled the room. Alex motioned for the women to make use of the water, and the lass poured water over the older woman's hands as she scrubbed them clean. Not making the mistake of approaching the elder, Alex offered a thick length of linen to the lass who passed it along.

Jean bustled in, wiping her hands on her apron, face flush with either haste or perhaps her work in the kitchen. Drawing to a halt, she surveyed the two women with a raised brow.

Alex gestured to his guests. "I found this pair beset by three men on the pier," he said, moving to his chair behind the enormous desk.

"I believe *that* one must have disagreed with their offer," Jean retorted, giving the older woman a skeptical look. The woman's chin lifted a notch, anger flashing across her face. Jean's eyes widened, unaccustomed to any show of disrespect.

"'Twas less than honorable," Alex replied, his lips twitching downward in displeasure—more for the act he'd caught the men in than for any impoliteness from the beleaguered woman. She would be accorded time to recover.

He sat, leaning against the comfortable leather-bound frame. "The two men who still live reside in the dungeon. Awaiting hanging for their offenses."

"And what is to be *their* fate?" Jean asked, inclining her head toward the women.

"'Tis up to them, but they have my vow of protection and I offered them work here—pending yer approval."

Jean's face softened, exposing her soft heart too often hidden beneath her bustling no-nonsense manner. "What's yer name, lass?" she asked. "Ye are welcome here."

The women exchanged looks, and the younger, again clutching the other's arm, ventured an answer. "I am Aadny," she whispered. She turned her worshipful gaze to the older woman at her side.

The elder lifted her chin. "I am Hanna, of the village of Hällstein on the Isle of Mull. The village and my family were destroyed, thanks to yer Scottish king."

Her voice, harsh with anger and grief, did not disguise her Norse accent, one Alex knew well. "*Jeg er lei meg*," he offered, though how a simple apology would make amends for what she'd endured, he did not know.

Both women startled.

"I speak some Norse," he said. "My business demands fluency in languages."

A serving lass appeared in the doorway. With a bob of her head, she held up a handful sturdy brown wool. "For the ladies, Laird," she said, slipping Hanna and Aadny a quick glance from the corners of her eyes.

Jean took the gowns. With a firm, motherly hand, she gathered Aadny to her side. "I'll have ye in a hot tub and clean clothes in no time."

"Have the healer take a look at Hanna's arm, if you please. I would rather not find her in bed with a raging fever in a day or two."

Jean sent Alex a brisk nod, "Leave it to me, Laird. I'll have the healer attend her. I'm certain I have lodging and work for them both."

With a twitch of her skirts, she led the women from the room. As the door closed behind them, Alex turned to the clutter on his desk, wanting very much to leave it behind and follow the women, anxious to see Hanna was well-cared for.

With a wry shake of his head, he dismissed the urge, having no need to embroil himself with one of the many refugees arriving at MacLean Castle daily.

But the peculiar desire he'd felt the first time he saw her, dagger dripping blood, her pale face and hair speckled with the dark spatter, a fierce Valkyrie defending a young lass's honor, floated through his chest again. Heat tightened his chest and loins.

Though presented with acceptable lasses, should he decide to take another wife, he'd found the one woman of whom no MacLean clan elder would approve.

Alex sighed. Jean would care for the woman. Perhaps it was best he dismissed from his mind the golden-haired Valkyrie with the wounded eyes.

Chapter Seven

Hanna ignored Jean's chatter as she submerged herself in the wooden tub. The water could have been as cold as the Strait of Mull for all the attention she paid to such minor details. It irked her to accept hospitality from Laird MacLean, and she did not trust his motives or those of the people around her. They were Scots—wild and uncivilized. Enemy to the Norse.

Hands gently gathered her hair and she gritted her teeth to keep from showing her revulsion. Water ran over her head and fingers massaged soap scented with rosemary into her hair and scalp. Hanna's stomach clenched at the kindness and she gripped the edges of the tub, using the dull pain to keep her shattered heart from betraying her.

Jean clucked her tongue. "I have need of a lass to help with the children. Aadny will suit." She motioned to Hanna. "Freya will help ye finish yer bath and show ye about. If ye have further need, send someone to find me." With a rustle of skirts, keys to the castle clanking at her waist, Jean hurried from the room, Aadny a silent shadow at her heels.

The door clicked shut and silence descended. Water sluiced the soap from Hanna's hair and she leaned forward, taking a square of cloth from the table and lathering it with more of the scented soap. Scrubbing vigorously, she erased the evidence of the past two days.

After a final rinse, the other woman spread Hanna's hair across her shoulders to begin drying and rose to her feet, wiping her hands on her apron.

"'Tis no Scots name ye bear," Hanna noted. The other woman, her hair a slightly darker gold than Hanna's, nodded.

"I, too, am a refugee. I arrived here little more than a sennight past." She lifted troubled eyes to meet Hanna's gaze. "Ye will find safety here. And acceptance."

"Acceptance?" Hanna drew back in horror. She could not envision a place among Scots where she, a Norsewoman, would be accepted. Their past was too stormy, the recent attacks on the Norse villages too bloody.

"The laird is a fair man, the work is not onerous, and after a time, ye will discover the people here are friendly." Freya's lips thinned. "'Tis best ye forget your past. Make a new life for yourself."

"Ye have not forgotten." Hanna's words did not question what she knew to be the truth.

Freya shook her head. "I will help ye dress and show ye to your duties. My life as a Norsewoman is over. I have made peace with myself. Ye would do well to consider yourself a Scot, now."

Hanna's blood fired in her veins. Not for all the peace in Scotland would she consider herself a Scot. She was Norse, and Clan MacLean would soon remember it as well.

She dressed quickly, slipping her dagger in her sleeve when Freya's attention was diverted, then followed the woman to the kitchen. Her duties were quickly explained, and she set to chopping vegetables, her eyes scanning the busy room, ears tuning to the high-pitched chatter.

The sight of a girl near her daughter Signy's age, cheeks rosy in the glow of the massive fireplace where she tended the cook fire, made Hanna's heart stop. Pushing the fierce longing past the grief clogging her throat, Hanna dragged her gaze to the women nearest her. Their actions spoke of long practice. Their voices, however, rose excitedly, and Hanna realized this evening's meal was more than a simple gathering.

"'Tis time he wed," declared a buxom older woman to Hanna's right, her bosom swaying as her hands firmly kneaded pastry dough.

"'Twould dash Agnes' hopes, it would," quipped the woman across the wooden table as she gave the woman next to her a dig with an elbow.

"He needs an older, more experienced lass to warm his bed," the one named Agnes retorted. "He'd cold comfort enough afore his wife died."

"Dinnae speak ill of the dead," the first woman admonished. "The woman did her duty."

"Aye, but with only a wee lass to show for it." Agnes clucked her tongue and bent to her work.

"Our Agnes has a soft spot for our laird, she does," Hanna's nearest neighbor confided, her eyes twinkling. "A verra soft spot!"

Agnes' cheeks flared bright pink. "I havenae slept with him," she croaked, clearly sensitive about her feelings for the MacLean laird.

The elder woman dusted the flour from her hands with an air of finality. "One of the lasses here tonight will, mark my words. 'Tis a bevy of bonny maids awaiting to give him the heir he needs, his bright wee lass notwithstanding." She flashed Hanna a look. "'Tis the reason for our extra work today. Laird MacLean has finally settled in from his travels and the elders have arranged the bonniest of our lasses to tempt him to remarry."

A dark-haired girl, likely no more than five or six summers old, skipped into the room, angling unerringly for the large preparation table, her nose tilted up as if scenting the air. Her eyes danced merrily as she approached the older woman.

"Lachina, are the pasties ready?" Her piping voice wheedled playfully, her tiny fingers dragged down the woman's rolled sleeve and tapped against the flour patterning her lower arms.

Lachina fisted one hand on an ample hip. "Ye know they are, *a leanbh*," she said, a broad smile on her face. She wagged a finger at the girl. "And ye also know I'll not spoil yer supper by giving ye one beforehand. Off with ye, now. 'Tis a good broth ye're needin', not an extra pasty."

Lachina ladled berries onto the rounds of dough, folded the pastry once, then placed them on a platter. With a pointed look at the lass, she carted the uncooked pasties away. The girl dabbled a fingertip in the flour scattered across the table, then turned to the other women.

Hanna caught her breath at the longing in the girl's eyes. Wide and dark, they were the opposite of her daughter's, but something about the child held Hanna's interest. Dark hair escaped willy-nilly from the braid down her back, and a raveled thread marked the edge of one sleeve. The hem of her gown was inches above her sturdy but stained boots, and Hanna wondered if she'd dressed herself that morning.

An orphan, mayhap? Or the youngest child in a large family, dressed in hand-me-downs and not missed until bedtime if her chores were completed? Against her better judgement, Hanna laid her knife on the chopping block and wiped her hands on her apron.

"Is your belly empty?" she asked, fighting the urge to get too close, yet unable to deny the lure of the forlorn girl. The child nodded quickly.

"Aye. And I never—hardly ever," she corrected herself, "get one of Cook's best pasties." She sent Hanna a virtuous look. "I try to eat my vegetables, truly I do!" Her face fell. "But Peigi doesnae always agree."

Hanna imagined an older sister, vexed with the care of a child scarcely old enough to care for herself, imposing strict restrictions on the girl. She strode to the cooling rack near the ovens where the already baked pasties rested, beckoning the girl to her side. Slipping a scrap of linen around a robust pasty, she handed it to the child.

"Do not burn your mouth, and be certain to eat everything on your trencher at supper." She patted the girl's head, smoothing strands of thick black hair from her face.

The child nodded. "Thank ye!" She cocked her head to one side. "Ye are new here, aye?"

Hanna nodded, sudden alarm prickling along her skin. She hadn't meant to attract notice, and yet the bright eyes of this girl seemed to notice much.

"I know everyone in the kitchen. I'm Gillian. What's yer name? Would ye be my friend?"

"I am Hanna," she replied, seeking to halt the child's chatter. "And I must get back to my duties. Do not tell anyone of the pastie."

"Och, I willnae," the child assured her, eyes dancing merrily. "'Tis certain Peigi wouldnae let me have another!"

With a glance back at Hanna and a wave of her hand, the girl scurried between the tables and through the kitchen door. Lachina strode to Hanna's side.

"Her da will have his hands full once that one is of age," she noted with a heavy sigh. "God bless his soul."

* * *

Alex stared at the young women interspersed down the tables with various family members in attendance. Some smiled openly, some fluttered glances from beneath lowered eyelids. All were comely. All were young.

"Remind me whose idea this was?" he invited Edan, biting his lip against a scowl. The last thing he needed was a concerted effort to entice him to remarry. Once had been enough, God rest Annag's long-suffering soul. He'd spent long months aboard ship and in foreign countries, sampling what was offered. He'd be damned before he was shackled by duty again.

"A few of the elders still believe ye should remarry and produce an heir," Edan replied. He swept his gaze over the crowd. "Plenty for ye to choose from."

"They're young enough to be my daughters," Alex snorted in disgust. "I dinnae see why we cannae settle on Arbela's son—or even Gillian's husband once she is of age." He made a vague gesture with one hand. "This is ridiculous."

Edan rose and bent near. "Try a few out, Laird. Ye dinnae have to keep them."

With a broad grin, Edan strode away, leaving Alex to his plight.

To Alex's relief, Gillian streaked across the room before any of the more ambitions fathers could step to his table, skillfully dodging her nurse's efforts to stop her. Her dancing eyes echoing her grin of triumph, Gillian dove into Alex's lap as he scooted his chair back from the table. She planted a resounding kiss to his cheek then settled against him, surveying the simpering mass of maidenhood with all the subtle confidence of a well-loved six-year-old.

She stuck her thumb in her mouth and wiggled her shoulders more firmly against Alex. "They're staring, Da." She attempted a whisper around her abbreviated digit, but attained only a rasping quality, the volume loud enough to carry.

Alex smothered a laugh. "Aye, *leannan*," he replied, leaning his mouth close to her ear, her black hair tickling his nose. "None are as bonny as ye."

Gillian jerked upright and removed her thumb. "They're staring at *ye*," she corrected him with a frown.

He nodded sagely. "I'll wager they cannae believe such a bonny lass has such an auld, *crepit* da."

His daughter sighed. "Ye arenae auld," she reassured him. "Ye have only a wee bit of gray hair, and Auntie Bela has lots more gray hair than ye." She leaned her cheek against Alex's chest, her eyes observing the dwindling crowd.

"I imagine I will gray as ye grow. And I wouldnae repeat that about Auntie Bela's hair if I were ye," Alex said, grinning as he imagined his sister's response to Gillian's truthful remark. He looked forward to the years ahead with his precocious daughter. Bright, bonny, and self-assured, she reminded him mightily of her Auntie Bela, and Alex wondered how his da had survived his sister's clever skills as a child.

He nudged Gillian's elbow. "They are certain ye need a ma and have come to see if they could stomach living with me. We're a pair, ye know."

Gillian's head tilted in interest. "I dinnae need a ma," she declared. "Do ye wish a wife?"

Her nose wrinkled with her question, and Alex swallowed a laugh. "I dinnae believe so," he replied. "But if I change my mind, we will pick one out together."

"I like *her*," Gillian said, sitting forward and pointing to a woman clearing one of the tables. "She's nice."

Alex followed his daughter's gaze, startled to discover his Valkyrie from earlier wiping down the worn boards. It was unlikely he would have remarked her appearance had Gillian not pointed her out. Her hair, pulled back from her face and twisted around her head in a thick braid, glistened gold in the torchlight. Her movements were concise, with the grace of a lean lioness, and he found himself wishing he'd seen her take down the ruffian in the alley that morning.

His lips quirked in a half-grin. *What a bloody thought to have of a woman I scarcely know—and who could stand trial for murder, should I wish it.* His gaze lingered on the woman's—Hanna, wasn't it?—slender back, recalling her almost feral attitude earlier. Such a difference a bath and change of clothes made. His smile kicked up a notch and a purely male interest rose.

Giving Gillian a nudge from his lap, he rose. "Why dinnae we speak to yer new friend?"

Chapter Eight

Hanna slanted a glance to the head table, taken aback to see the dark-haired child she'd met earlier curled in the laird's lap. Her heart missed a beat. The girl's easy, assured nature should have alerted her, but she'd been taken in by the child's sweet nature and untidy appearance to heed the warning signs. Now, dressed in a fetching gown of fine wool—not a tattered or bespattered hem in sight—she radiated the charm of an indulged laird's daughter.

Gillian. The MacLean's daughter. A low rage simmered in her belly. The Scot's daughter lived, whilst Signy lay beneath a pile of charred rubble. Darkness hemmed the edge of her vision, as she pondered the possible change in her plans for revenge.

It would be easy to strike at the laird through his daughter—and how fitting his loss should echo hers. Hanna's nostrils flared in distaste.

She snatched a platter from the table, slamming the trenchers she'd gathered onto the broad surface. Gripping the handles with white knuckles, Hanna braced against the overwhelming waves of grief.

It mattered to no one when my daughter died. Or my son. No one hesitated to destroy my family, my life. Nay, the cursed Scots relished the task.

Tears slipped from burning eyes and she blinked to clear her vision as she bore her burdens to the kitchen.

Something tugged at her skirt.

"Hanna?" a small voice chirped.

Hanna whirled. Her platter slammed against a broad chest mere inches away, and the trenchers crashed to the floor. She released the platter, freeing her hands, the tip of a dagger appearing magically from her sleeve. Her gaze slid from the child to the man immediately in front of her. He grabbed her forearm in a bruising grip, immobilizing her, rendering her threat ineffective. His dark eyes pierced hers, reminding her the man did not succeed as laird by being weak.

The tense line of his jaw echoed the taut muscles of his body, weight poised slightly forward, ready to counter her next move. Forcing back her anger, she relaxed, tearing her gaze away to indicate at least partial surrender. His grip loosened, though she knew she'd bear the marks for a few days, yet he did not completely release her. His touch burned her skin. His half-step closed the remaining distance between them, trapping the threat of the dagger between them.

"Are ye well?" he asked, his voice sliding smooth as aged whisky through her ears.

Hanna eyed him warily. Her heart raced. "I was told ye did not tolerate abuse of women." With a supreme effort, she kept her tone barely within the range of civil. Something flashed in his eyes, but was quickly gone.

"'Tis understandable ye wish to protect yerself. And fortunate none has seen the glint of steel between us." A moment of tense silence slid past. "Put away yer dagger," Laird MacLean growled. "Yer safety is assured. And the mess easily put to right."

The dagger disappeared into the narrow sheath beneath her sleeve, Hanna's hesitancy brief and unremarked. She remained of half a mind to plunge the blade into his chest and be finished with her torment. Joining her family in the afterlife held great appeal, and she'd no doubt she'd not last long once her vengeance was sated. But a quick death for the laird weighed against his lifetime of the same sorrow and loss she felt? She needed more time to plan her revenge.

He straightened, releasing her as he gestured to a passing lad. "Gather what has slid beneath the tables," he ordered. "We cannae have Hanna crawling where a lad goes best."

"I apologize," Laird MacLean said, turning his attention back to her. "Wee Gillian said she met ye earlier, and I wished to ask how ye fare. 'Twas not my intent to startle ye."

"I am well," she bit out, furious to owe her current home and food to a despised Scot. "I will return to my duties."

The laird smiled. Hanna shoved away an impulse to return the gesture, refusing to let the light crinkles at the outer corners of his eyes sway her opinion of him. He was the king's man, and therefore aligned with those who had destroyed her family and friends. A bonny smile and friendly manner could not change the tilt of his allegiance.

She vowed his smile would soon be a thing of the past.

* * *

Alex's gaze followed the Norsewoman's retreat, her shoulders square, head high. He sighed. Too many people—widows, orphans—fled the Isles, seeking refuge from the battle between the two kings. A few escaped just ahead of the culling axe—most arrived bearing blood-stained clothing and dark hearts.

Something about Hanna tugged at him. Her grief was fresh, yet she pursued her tasks without hesitation. She carried herself like a queen, even as she blotted food stains from the scarred tables. He'd seen her quick to defend a helpless lass, knew her to be capable of violence. Yet Gillian had seen something more amenable in Hanna and liked her—perhaps there was a more welcoming side to his

Valkyrie.

His Valkyrie? His cock twitched agreeably.

"Do ye like her, Da?" Gillian asked, interrupting his thoughts.

Hanna disappeared into the hall to the kitchen and Alex reluctantly pulled his gaze to his daughter. "I believe Hanna is a good woman," he said. "And her heart is heavy. Go easy on her, aye?"

"Och," Gillian said, dismissing his concern airily. "She needs me. Mayhap ye, as well."

* * *

Hanna tossed fitfully on her pallet in the hall. Unused to sleeping amid so many, each breath, each snore, every rustle of straw combined to scatter what little semblance of peace she'd managed to pull together after her exhausting day.

She lay awake long into the night, musing over the past hours. Laird MacLean's mercy was a bitter dreg to swallow. She felt no remorse over the killing of the man at the dock who'd arrogantly thrust his attentions on a young girl. And it confused her when he'd sentenced the other two to their deaths, meting out impartial justice.

She'd meant to make an example of the Scot. Hurt him as she'd been. Force him to understand the depth of her pain, loss that bit so deep nothing but her own death could end it. A small voice she did not wish to hear whispered Laird MacLean was a merciful man, and wronging him was not honorable. Hanna closed her eyes and pulled the thin blanket higher over her shoulders and fell into a troubled slumber.

Chapter Nine

Alex scraped a hand through his hair in frustration, caught by Gillian as he perused the list of provisions for the *Porpoise*. Though it would be some weeks before he was due to meet the king, his daughter refused to be put off. "I cannae take ye with me this time, Gillian. Dinnae fash. I will only be gone a sennight or so."

"I want to go, Da!" she insisted, dark eyes brimming with tears. Alex inhaled deeply. This trip would be no exciting travel full of different ports, and merchants hawking wares to delight a young girl's fancy. It likely meant a long, drawn-out siege, and his hopes for a week's time away seemed overly optimistic.

"I know ye do, lass," he soothed. "And I would be pleased to have ye with me—another time."

"I want to go with ye *this* time," Gillian pouted.

"'Tis no trip for a wee lass," Alex replied. "I will take ye to the dock and see the *Porpoise* today—before I leave," he added, hoping the bribe would be successful.

"I dinnae wish to stay behind. Peigi isnae well, and I dinnae have anyone when ye are gone." This time her lower lip slid forward as the corners drifted downward.

Alex's resolve slipped a notch. He scooped Gillian into his arms. "Battle isnae a place for a lass, and I will be too busy to attend ye." He chucked her beneath her chin, coaxing a hint of a smile as she ducked her head. Alex tried a new tactic.

"Mayhap we should spend an hour or two thinking of a name for yer new puppy."

Gillian's face lit as she jerked upright. "Da! Do I truly have a puppy?"

"I think ye are old enough to have the care of one. Would it please ye?"

"Och, aye!" She nodded vigorously. "I will take the best care ever! I will even give him my carrots," she added solemnly.

Alex threw back his head, laughter erupting. "Ye will eat yer own carrots, Gillian MacLean. Puppies dinnae eat them."

Gillian shrugged, blithely unconcerned to be caught in her ploy to avoid the one vegetable she disliked most. Setting his daughter from his lap, Alex took her hand.

"Let's see if he is in the kennel."

Gillian skipped beside him, and his heart soared at her cheerfulness. The past year had been difficult for the lass, but he was pleased to see her spirits blooming.

They approached the kennel, Gillian's excitement doubling, then trebling, until she clung to his arm, scarcely able to refrain from jumping up and down.

"What is the first lesson around animals, lass?" Alex asked.

Gillian immediately sobered. "I dinnae wish to frighten him," she whispered. "Am I being good, now?"

"Aye, ye are perfect," he replied. Unlatching the half-door, he pushed it open. Gillian's hands flew to cover her mouth, her eyes wide and shining.

"Och, Da! He's so furry!"

"A wee gift from yer Auntie Bela," Alex said. "The puppy's ma is one of her Aidi dogs, and its da is a deerhound. I believe he will be rather large when he grows up." Alex eyed the puppy's enormous feet.

"I will name him Bjarne," Gillian announced. "He will be big as a bear!"

Alex's laughter rumbled. "I believe ye are right."

Gillian fell to her knees, squealing happily as the puppy dashed over to her and plopped into her lap, raining sloppy kisses on her cheeks. "Can he sleep with me?" she asked as soon as she was able to cuddle the puppy in her arms.

Alex sighed. "We will have to ask Peigi. She will have charge of ye whilst I am gone. And that means of wee Bjarne, as well."

"Och, Da, I dinnae think Peigi likes dogs." Gillian's face fell. "And she isnae well. Can someone else be my nurse whilst ye are away?"

Her wistful voice tugged at Alex's heart. It was true Peigi was strict with the child, but Alex could count on her to guard his daughter with her life. Though he knew Gillian saw her nurse as a bit of a dragon, she always had the child's good at heart.

"Mayhap just this once," Alex reluctantly replied, casting through his memory for someone to replace Peigi for the week or so he would be gone. "I dinnae know who 'twould be, though I agree Peigi isnae helpful if she isnae well."

Gillian's face beamed. "Let's go see Hanna. I think she likes puppies."

A spark of interest ran through Alex. "An excellent idea, Daughter. I believe we should check on Hanna."

* * *

Laughter swirled near the kitchen door, punctuated with high-pitched giggles, snagging Hanna's attention. Laird MacLean, in the act of taking a bite of a pastry, halted, his face red, his daughter hopping from one foot to the other.

"I caught ye!" she chanted merrily. "Cook likes ye, too!"

Laird MacLean stuffed the last bite in his mouth and quickly chewed and swallowed. "'Tis not likely to ruin my supper, lassie," he declared, planting a hearty kiss on the child's upturned cheek. "I grew bored waiting for ye to walk yer wee puppy, and feared I would die of hunger before ye arrived."

"Da!" Gillian protested. "Bjarne needed me."

The laird looked at the puppy dangling in his daughter's arms. "Have ye decided to bring the puppy into the castle, then?"

Gillian nodded vigorously. "He will be a good boy. Ye'll see."

Hanna shrank away, wishing for a shadowed corner in which to disappear. She did not want to see the happy father and daughter. Or the puppy with the slow-wagging tail and soulful eyes. Too many memories, refreshing her sorrow, tugging at her heart in inexplicable ways.

"There's Hanna," Gillian declared with a tilt of her head in Hanna's direction. She hefted the puppy in her arms and strode to Hanna's side. "Do ye like dogs?" She lifted the puppy a bit higher with a shrug of her shoulder to show him off. "Bjarne and I are going to be great friends."

Bewildered, Hanna stared at the puppy. "Bjarne?"

"Aye. He's furry as a bear. His real name is Torbjorn, which means *Thor's bear* in Norse. But I just call him Bjarne."

The child's matter-of-fact voice startled Hanna. "Ye speak Norse?" She glanced at the laird for confirmation. Laird MacLean grinned and Hanna's heart skipped a beat.

"The lass has an ear for languages." He glanced about the room. "And as it appears we have as many in this kitchen who speak Norse as we do Scots or Gaelic, she had no reason not to learn."

"But, ye are aligned with King Alexander . . . ." Hanna shook her head, fearing some sort of trap. "I do not understand."

"The king has his plans," the laird agreed smoothly. "But I have no concern for yers so long as they dinnae interfere with yer duties and dinnae put me or my clan in an untenable position."

Fury sparked in Hanna. Her family had fallen to men using

King Alexander's name for their conquest. "Your king has violated his agreement with Norway."

Laird MacLeod remained silent for several seconds. "King Alexander has concluded he and Norway are at an impasse. As such, he is prepared to unify Scotland by the most expedient means at his disposal."

"He has signed our death warrants!" Hanna burst out, unable to stop her words. "King Haakon is too far away . . .." She bit her lip against the outpouring.

Laird MacLean stepped closer. "Mayhap we should make time to discuss yer thoughts another time," he murmured, pitching his voice lower, indicating the attention they'd garnered in the kitchen.

Hanna shrugged. "I have no thoughts," she replied, turning back to the cutting board.

"I believe ye do," the laird replied, his voice silky smooth over the steel edge of command.

The puppy whined, apparently no longer complacent in Gillian's grip. He wriggled, forcing the child to release him. His fat paws scrabbled on the stone floor as he spied a tabby cat just settling in a patch of sunlight in the doorway to the garden. With a yip of challenge, Bjarne bounded over as the enraged cat arched it back, hissing and spitting a warning to the heedless pup.

"Bjarne! No!" Gillian cried, darting after him. The cat leapt onto a nearby table, causing the women working there to shriek in protest. Bjarne skidded to a halt, his youthful lack of coordination sending him crashing into the table legs. A crockery bowl, placed too close to the edge, plummeted to the floor, shattering on impact. Gillian scooped up her puppy, scolding him roundly. Laird MacLean faced Hanna, his assessing gaze gone.

"Please join me in my solar."

Hanna slowly settled the kitchen knife on the table and wiped her hands on a scrap of cloth hanging from her belt. She followed him down the passage, keeping a goodly distance between them, her skin fairly rippling with the sensation of being so near the MacLean laird. Her arm flexed slightly, checking the weight of the small dagger in her sleeve.

Laird MacLean slung himself into a chair near the hearth and indicated Hanna to do the same. She refused, remaining rooted to the planks near the door, glaring at him from beneath her lashes.

The laird leaned his head back on the chair. "I willnae bite."

"Nay," Hanna replied. "Ye have done much more than that."

He rolled his head in her direction. "What have I done?"

"Ye are Scot. I am Norse," Hanna snarled, stepping inside the room, head up, subservient attitude gone. "I will not place myself in harm's way."

"Ye are under my protection," he replied with a scowl. "And ye will answer my questions."

Hanna flinched to recognize how truly precarious her position was. Without male protection, few men would hesitate to use her as they wished. And the clan chief owned more right than most. Hanna ground her teeth, certain he would not be bested as easily as the man on the docks. She could flee, fight, or acquiesce. Which would it be?

The laird again waved her to the chair across from him and this time Hanna accepted. She perched on the edge of the seat, hands in her lap, her thumb stroking the length of the sheath hidden beneath her sleeve.

"Relax," he advised. "A short break will do ye good."

Hanna lifted a brow, inviting him to forego the pleasantries and ask his questions.

"I apologize for my abruptness earlier," he said. "Ye seem to react to everything I say as though I have wronged ye. Has anyone here attempted to harm ye?"

To Hanna's surprise, a smile blossomed on the laird's face. "I say *attempted*, for I am well aware how ye would state yer refusal, and to my knowledge, there has been no rash of injuries requiring the healer's care. Ye are a dangerous woman, Hanna of Hällstein."

His eyes narrowed. "Speaking of the healer, how is yer arm?"

"It does not keep me from my duties." Hanna gathered her skirts and prepared to rise. "Did ye have other questions for me, Laird? In case ye had not noticed, I am also a *busy* woman."

"Do ye have other family nearby?"

The question, though expected, took the breath from her. Hanna swallowed hard, willing her lungs to work properly.

"I do not have kin I may shelter with, Laird," she replied. "My parents' village was disbanded over a year ago in another of King Alexander's purges. I have lost track of them, and truly do not know if they still live."

The laird leaned forward, his gaze intent. "Please call me Alex," he requested. His words again took her off guard. His invitation was too personal and Hanna could not allow the intimacy.

She found her voice again, though it slipped brittle between her teeth as she forced herself to speak aloud what had happened only three nights prior. "My family—my husband and two children—were killed in a raid by Scots, and our village burned to the ground."

Alex shook his head. "This has gone much too far. My father swore allegiance to Scotland's king when we came here nearly thirty years ago. It was an expedient move, as he'd hoped to set up a shipping trade at ports along the Scottish coast. My ancestors, however, aligned with the King of the Isles, and thus we were both accepted and considered suspect by both parties."

"I know of ye as the king's man, though we have . . . *had* traded with ye a few times in the past. It appears ye have a reputation for fairness from both sides."

"And yet ye speak of my reputation as though it pains ye."

Hanna grew still. "My home was attacked by soldiers under your king's orders," she continued as her throat constricted and her palms grew sweaty. "We were given the opportunity to swear allegiance to the Scottish king, foreswearing all ties to King Haakon and the King of the Isles." She bit her lip, then continued. "*After* they killed the men and torched the long house—and those sheltering inside it."

Alex's gaze narrowed and he tilted his head to one side. "What would ye have said, had ye been given time to answer their demand before such carnage?" he asked.

Hanna leveled an icy gaze at him. "I would have refused."

Chapter Ten

Aadny's pale, slender fingers stroked through Gillian's dark hair, smoothing the sections into a braid. "I am happy Peigi asked me to help care for ye," she said. "Ye remind me of my little sister." Aadny tweaked Gillian's ear. "Ye are a *livlig jente*, as she was."

Hanna paid scant heed to Aadny's words. It had been two days since an ailing Peigi had asked for Aadny's assistance, and Hanna found the proximity with the laird's daughter exhausted her emotions. Aadny still stuck close to Hanna's side, as if by saving her life, they were now forever linked, and Gillian had joined their tiny circle. It was impossible to watch Aadny and Gillian together and plot revenge.

I cannot avenge myself on an innocent. The thought warred constantly in her head, and only Gillian's cheerful laughter and Bjarne's antics had the power to quiet the passion revenge stirred in her breast.

At what point do my actions determine the truth of my heart? Hanna could not deny the pain of loss, the terrible, empty space in her chest that often stopped her breath. She had killed men, in both battle and in self-defense. But this act she contemplated was not the same. Gillian's death would force the same grief upon the MacLean Laird. But it would not lessen hers, and it would not bring honor to Signy or Sten's memory.

She stared at Aadny's hands, mesmerized by their slow, repetitive movement. She imagined the feel of baby-fine hair beneath her own fingers, silk rasping against work-roughened skin. A pang of longing shot through her.

"Hanna?" Gillian's voice piped through the pain. "Will ye tell me a story tonight?"

Hanna released her breath and took a step into the present. "I do not think I know any stories," she lied. "I will take Bjarne outside once more and then ye should sleep."

"Did ye not tell stories to yer children?" Gillian asked, peering over her shoulder as Aadny secured the bottom of the braid.

The question caught Hanna off-guard. "My children?"

"Do ye not have bairns?" Gillian's question was innocent, but Hanna could scarcely answer, so tight was the band about her heart.

"I believe Hanna does not wish to speak of it," Aadny whispered to Gillian. The child's face fell. After a moment, she rose and went to Hanna, encircling her knees with her arms.

"My brothers and sisters died, too," she said solemnly as she buried her face against Hanna's skirt. "So did my ma."

Hanna's chest rose and fell rapidly, the only rhythm which kept her tears at bay. Her hands fisted, opened, fisted again. Her knees shook, and she lowered to the floor, pulling Gillian into her arms. Aadny sank beside them, her sobs blending with Gillian's.

Completely empty and bereft as her thoughts of revenge fled, Hanna let hot tears trail down her cheeks.

* * *

Alex viewed Gillian's friendship with Hanna with mild suspicion. Though the woman had been at MacLean Castle for less than a sennight, it was easy to see the child was besotted with both Aadny—understandable as the lass was more like an elder sister than a nurse—and Hanna. Though Hanna appeared to keep Gillian at arm's length.

If he was truthful, Alex's interest in the Norsewoman was more personal. There were any number of young women—both Scots and

Norse—available to care for Gillian. But Alex found his attention pulled more and more in Hanna's direction. Even when his gaze met a cool, calculating look. What did Hanna contemplate?

His own curiosity knew no bounds. The golden glint of Hanna's hair, her sinewy grace, the piercing look of her dark green eyes, urged him to do more than watch. He wanted to touch her, spill her loosened braids across his hands, capture her interest, engage her wild, passionate nature. Perhaps Edan was right. No one would blink an eye if he took a lover.

The door to his solar opened a few inches and a shadow appeared in the lower half of the opening. Gillian stuck her head around the edge of the wood plank, her eyes wide with distress. Alex rose immediately.

"*Leannan*," he said. "What is wrong?"

"I made Hanna cry," she whimpered as she burrowed against him. He lifted her into his arms and carried her to one of the chairs by the hearth. He settled against the deep cushions and hugged her tight.

"Tell me what happened."

He got the story out of Gillian in sniffling bursts. Now that Hanna had retired for the night, leaving Aadny to sleep in Gillian's room, the child was overcome with remorse and sought Alex's reassurance.

"I am certain she does not believe ye meant to hurt her," Alex said. "She will feel better in the morn, as will ye. And now, I shudder to consider what Aadny will think if she wakes and finds ye gone."

Gillian's lips rounded. "Och, I dinnae think about her. Must I go back to my room? Can I sleep here?"

"I believe 'tis best I take ye back. Though I dinnae know if I would be welcome inside." He lowered his voice to a conspiratorial whisper. "Young lasses dinnae like to wake to find men in their room uninvited." He waggled his eyebrows and Gillian giggled.

She slid from his lap. "I will go back to my room." She placed her palms on his knees and leaned forward to plant a giant kiss on his cheek. "I wouldnae wish to frighten Aadny."

She giggled again, humor restored, and Alex opened his door, making a show of peering into the hall.

"All clear," he whispered. Gillian darted into the passage, her white sleep gown a pale flutter in the darkened hall. Alex watched until she reached her own door two rooms away. Gillian paused, then blew him a kiss before stepping inside.

Alex listened for the snick of her door closing, then leaned against the door frame, pensive.

So, that is what keeps Hanna from falling under Gillian's spell. The wound is still too new, too raw for her to consider giving her heart to the child. Perhaps Gillian was right after all. Perhaps Hanna needed Gillian—and Alex, too.

Hand on the latch, he started to pull the door closed. But a figure paused at the head of the stairs then bolted across the hall to the stairs leading to the parapet. After a moment's hesitation, Alex followed.

* * *

Hanna closed the door of the tiny room beneath the rafters where she and Aadny quartered. As their stay lengthened, Jean had assigned them the small space rather than remain scattered about in the great hall. Two pallets, piled with patched quilts and topped with faded woolen blankets, took up much of the floor space, though as the bitter night air was wont to slip between the cracks in the wooden floor—the quality of the planks at this level woefully unable to form tight seams—and between the stone walls and the roofing, made small rooms preferable to larger ones that were harder to heat.

Usually, she and Aadny brought heated stones to bed with them, and occasionally, when Hanna could manage it, a smaller stone to heat water in a small, dented basin for a quick wash. But this night, alone and heartsore, Hanna sank onto her pallet, oblivious to the cold.

I cannot do this. My heart does not wish to inflict pain on innocents. Laird MacLean is not the man who commanded the men who burned my village. I can no more hurt Gillian than I could my own child.

Something sharp twisted in her gut and she nearly cried out at the unexpected pain.

My family is gone. Yet I live. She stared into the darkness. *Why? For what reason does God keep me here? What have I done to deserve such torment? How can I endure the pain?*

Wind whispered beneath the eaves and a shutter banged against the stone—an empty sound that resonated deep inside Hanna.

Suddenly, the darkness was too much and Hanna leapt from her pallet, heedless of the blanket that tangled about her ankles. She stumbled to the door and yanked it open, met by the dim glow of a guttered torch. With blind determination, she proceeded through the passage and down the stairs to the landing one level below, where the laird and his family slept. A door at the end of the hall opened into a narrow stair to the parapet. Hanna made the ascent and fled to the edge of the stone wall.

Fresh air rushed over her skin, prickling it into henflesh. Her cheekbones and nose chilled instantly. Hanna drew a deep, shuddering breath and stared over the landscape arrayed in black and white.

Trees disclosed their shadowed secrets beneath the bright light of the moon, revealing the creatures of the night as they bustled about. The air, scented with summer flowers and damp earth, filled her nose and lungs with the aroma of life. An owl called from his perch high in a tree. Instantly all movement on the ground ceased, life suspended as the predator's threat loomed over them.

The moonlight reflected in the owl's eyes fascinated Hanna. The feathered hunter surveyed his territory for long minutes, then, with a silent whoosh of powerful wings, he glided into the forest, releasing the creatures below from death one more time.

Hanna's breath slipped on a long sigh and she did not startle when a warm weight settled onto her shoulder. Her gaze dropped to the hand, black hair springing from the scuffed knuckles. Slowly lifting her eyes, she met Laird MacLean's troubled gaze.

"Halt, Hanna," he whispered. "This isnae how ye beat them."

Chapter Eleven

"What do ye know of my misery," she demanded, husky voice filled with grief and anger. "There is naught left for me. Your king has killed me just as certain as the Scot who destroyed my family."

"I understand some of yer pain," Alex replied. "It empties ye, leaving ye a husk of what ye once were. Then, it fills ye with anger, full to bursting, and ye panic to realize ye are truly alone and all that once was good and right inside ye is now gone."

"I do not recognize myself," Hanna whispered.

"Because 'tis not ye. The man who killed yer family is to blame. But listen to me, Hanna. If ye do this thing, if ye leap from the wall, he will win. Without lifting a hand further, he will have won."

Hanna stared over the edge of the parapet. "Ye are but a man. What do ye know of a mother's grief?"

"A man, aye. But one who has experienced grief in many forms. The loss of a good friend in battle, of a father, and of a child in his mother's arms."

Hanna's attention slowly turned to him, her eyes dark with anguish, but her furrowed brow softened, giving him hope she was not lost to them yet.

"Would ye come with me?" he asked. "I know a quiet place where we can speak without interruption."

Breathing deeply, as though firming a decision, Hanna nodded, and Alex gently squeezed her hand, encouraging her to walk with him. He left her at the doorway to his chamber just long enough to grab a heavy cloak and a thick woolen blanket, grateful neither one of them had undressed for the night.

Alex led her through the great hall, the vast room lit only from the pale glow of the fire banked in the hearth. Snores punctuated with the occasional grunt covered the almost soundless tread of his and Hanna's feet as they passed among the sleepers.

Alex let go of Hanna's hand as he pushed one of the enormous doors open just enough to let them through. Nodding to the pair of guards standing at attention on the doorstep, he reclaimed her hand and led her across the yard to the small kirk abutting the outer wall of MacLean Castle. A large tree grew next to the building, casting its shadows over the kirkyard tucked behind a low stone fence.

He led her to a bench beneath the tree and covered the wooden surface with the blanket. Wordless, Hanna sank onto the seat, folding her hands in her lap, allowing Alex to wrap the cloak about her shoulders.

Mist rose about their feet, enveloping them. Had it not been for the faint scrape of booted feet on the parapet above, it would have been easy to imagine they were the only two people awake at that hour. He sat beside her.

I want to know everything about ye. Would she welcome his questions? Would she be honest? Would she tell him everything? Alex stared at the markers lined neatly behind the stone walls, anchored in white fog to the cold ground.

"I come here from time to time when I wish to think," Alex admitted. "Does it bother ye?"

"'Tis an interesting place to visit," she murmured, rousing with a deep sigh. "I can see why ye remain unmarried."

Alex snorted, unaccountable glee racing through him at Hanna's dry humor.

"Aye, the lassies prefer a livelier crowd."

Hanna tilted her head. "Why here?"

He dipped his head to a row of small crosses, a larger one in their midst. "'Tis where my family is buried."

"Your ancestors?"

Alex's throat constricted. "My bairns. And my wife."

Hanna's slow inhale mirrored Alex's sorrow. "Your daughter mentioned them."

"Aye. She told me about yer talk earlier this night. She was upset she made ye cry."

"I will speak to her," Hanna replied. "She is not to blame."

"Och, I told her so. And I'm fair certain she believed me. Though hearing it from ye would be good." Alex paused then leaned forward, resting his forearms on his thighs. He wanted to know more, but Hanna had already spoken more words—without rancor, nonetheless—to him than she had since arriving in Morvern. He decided to risk it. "Would ye tell me about yer family?"

Hanna did not answer, and after several silent moments, Alex feared he'd asked too much too soon. He carefully sought her hand, slow, taking care not to startle her. His fingers wound gently about hers, and Hanna's breath hitched. He gave her hand a squeeze and she returned the motion.

"My daughter Signy was twelve," she said. "The men came in the night—I woke to the dogs barking and as Torvald left our bed."

Hanna lifted her face to the moonlight and Alex's heart clenched at the bright stain of tears on her cheeks. "I sent her and the other girls and children to the hidden area beneath the long house. My son Sten would not go. Though he was but ten summers, he counted himself a man, and wished to defend his home."

A pre-dawn breeze drifted through the tree's branches above them, rattling the leaves like the whisper of approval.

"A braw young man," Alex commented. "A credit to ye and his da."

"I set him and a few of his friends to guard the door to the long house. 'Twas the only thing I could think of that would give them a sense of purpose yet keep them from the midst of the fight."

"Ye are a good woman, Hanna of Hällstein," Alex said. "'Twas an honorable choice."

"Yet it did not matter," she replied bitterly. "In the end, none survived."

Her shoulders shook. Alex angled toward her and laid a palm against the curve of her cheek. The damp of her tears unraveled his restraint and he gently pulled her head against his shoulder. Her body stiffened, and he whispered against her hair.

"Dinnae fash, *leannan*. I willnae hurt ye. Let yer tears fall. I dinnae know if 'twill help, but they are no good dammed up inside."

Hanna eased closer, her head a welcome weight against his shoulder. Alex held her until her shudders ceased and her silent tears had soaked through his leine. She pulled away, resuming her place next to him, her hand lingering in his. Alex closed the gap between them, his thigh meeting the length of hers through her skirts.

He squeezed her hand again. "Ye are a survivor, Hanna."

"But to what purpose?" she railed at him. "Of what purpose is this life of grief and despair? I wished to seek revenge, yet find I can do nothing." Her voice, heavy with the aftermath of her tears, wound about his heart.

"Did ye seek me out for revenge? Though 'twas not by my command yer family was destroyed, I confess surprise I havenae found your dagger in my ribs. As I have said before, ye are a formidable woman, Hanna."

Hanna stared at their hands. "I did not care who I harmed. I simply needed a Scot to hurt as much as I did. Seeking refuge with the MacDougall would have been safer, for none can breach the walls of Dunstaffnage Castle, and King Haakon has named him

King of the Isles." Her eyes traveled up Alex's arms, finally meeting his gaze.

"I know ye are not the person responsible for the deaths and the destruction of Hällstein. But ye are a Scot, and therefore my enemy."

"Och, Hanna, I am not yer enemy. 'Tis my hope ye will stay at MacLean Castle."

"Are ye in such need of kitchen staff ye solicit the aid of Norsewomen? Will that not anger your king?"

"The king has little say in who sleeps behind MacLean walls," Alex said. "I willnae succor rebellion, but those who truly seek refuge are welcome here." He leaned against the back of the bench. "My hopes that ye will remain here are a bit more personal."

* * *

Hanna stilled, measuring the import of his words. "What would ye have me do, Laird?"

"First, I would have ye call me Alex, as I have given ye leave to do before."

The weight of his large, calloused hands doubled. The beat of her heart picked up. Dread closed in on her like a trap. "'Tis not appropriate that I do so."

"I dinnae give a cricket's chance in a moor full of robins about the appropriateness of it. I wish ye to speak to me as an equal."

"I am not your equal."

"Och, I believe ye are. If ye had visited MacLean Castle on the arm of yer husband, ye would have been fed from the high table, and I would have welcomed ye with a kiss to the back of yer hand." He lifted her hand to his lips.

"I believe ye offered me a place in your kitchen rather than your dungeon," Hanna replied, her fingers curling as she battled the urge to snatch her hand away.

Alex shrugged and lowered her hand but did not release it. "Aye. I took yer measure then, and I have revised my opinion verra little since."

"Oh? And who do ye think I am? I have already told ye I came here planning revenge."

"Ye did," Alex agreed. "But I judged ye an honorable woman the day I met ye, and that hasnae changed. 'Tis my hope ye have abandoned the thought of vengeance. My heart grieves for yer loss, Hanna. But ye will learn to live with it in time."

"In time?" Hanna spat the words. "Time will fill the emptiness of my heart? Time will give me back what I had?"

"Nae. I am not so foolish to believe that. Like ye, I have lost those closest to me. I have buried three children, a father, and a wife. Though my loss was less brutal, we are not so unalike, Hanna."

"Have ye forgotten them? Has the ache eased?" Hanna flung her words at him, the bite of loss tearing through her.

"Nae. I willnae forget them, or the promise their lives held. Howbeit, sometimes I find the ache has eased."

A tiny flicker of hope kindled inside her. "Sometimes? What happens then?"

"From time to time, I find something of such beauty or such peace, that my heart is filled. In those moments, the ache leaves me."

Alex shifted on the bench, and Hanna flinched beneath the heat of his stare. She gazed at him, wondering if she'd ever find those moments of beauty and peace. Yet, something prickled at the margins of her grief, like threads loosening on a worn garment, easing its binding, allowing her to breathe more freely. To her surprise, his presence brought her comfort, the stroke of his thumb across the back of her hand light and undemanding.

"What else do ye wish of me?" Hanna pulled away. She did not want his touch, did not like to acknowledge it was human, kind. But she found her wariness of him lessening, and her anger perhaps a shade lighter.

"I want to see ye smile, Hanna. There is much I would do to have ye turn an honest smile on me."

"That may be more than I can bear," she said. "More than I can give ye."

Alex nodded. "Aye. For now. But, remember ye are safe here. And wanted."

She relapsed into scorn, fighting the compassion in his words. "Wanted? The skills of the kitchen staff are so woefully lacking?"

"Hanna, when ye find yerself willing, I would offer the warmth of my bed. 'Twill never be the condition of yer stay here, for that has no cost. I simply wish my intentions to be clear to ye."

Hanna recoiled as though slapped.

"Ye wish me to become your mistress?"

Chapter Twelve

Hanna paid little heed to the teasing and laughter from the women in the kitchen. She had worried Alex's proposition like a dog with a fresh bone for much of the remainder of the night once they'd parted company, and still could not decide if she was flattered or offended. With his reassurance he would not press her, Hanna had decided to remain—at least for a time. Aadny needed her as much as Gillian did. Dare she allow them to fill the vast hole in her heart? A twist of grief rose with the reminder she'd not have such days with her son or daughter again. Her hands faltered and she pulled in a deep steadying breath.

The woman next to her nudged her with her elbow, startling Hanna from her thoughts. "That one's set her sights on the laird and eager to warm his bed," she said, a grin across her face as she nodded at Agnes.

"And why not?" Agnes replied loftily, hearing the woman's comment. "I am young enough to birth an heir."

"And ye still have most of yer teeth!" another jested.

"Och, a pretty smile may draw him in, but 'tis not what keeps a man's interest!"

Laughter followed this bit of wisdom.

"What about ye, Hanna?"

"Aye, Hanna. Would ye seek the laird's favor?"

Hanna shook her head, wondering if the woman had the gift of sight. Surely the laird would not have spoken of their conversation to others. "Nae. I am Norse. Why should he seek me?" It was a good question—one she had been unable to answer.

"She'd as lief skewer him as swive him," Agnes grumbled, her eyes flashing as she sent Hanna a withering glare. Hanna raised an eyebrow in defiance.

"As would any woman approached where she does not invite," she replied.

Gillian wove through the room, her puppy trailing at her heels. She peered at the work tables, nose twitching—seeking pasties, no doubt. Lachina swung the child onto the table and handed her a bannock left from the morning meal, then tossed a freshly trimmed bone to Bjarne. Gillian munched her treat happily, swinging her legs back and forth, her interested gaze following the women's banter. Hanna sent a warning look to the women and talk turned to more mundane topics.

"What do ye plan this day," Hanna said, redirecting Gillian's thoughts. "Does your nurse encourage you to study?"

"Peigi isnae well and is napping. And I can read in three languages. I'd like to visit the *Alacrity* today," Gillian announced, biting into a second oatcake. A chunk dropped to the floor and Bjarne paused worrying his bone long enough to sniff out and devour the scrap. He searched the floor once more then resumed gnawing.

Hanna scraped chopped carrots into a large bowl. "Indeed? Why would a young girl care to traipse about a ship?" she asked, hoping the child was merely musing the day's possibilities. Hanna's memories of ships were not pleasant ones.

Gillian shrugged. "'Tis my da's ship and I picked her name. So, I 'spect she's partly mine as well. Da says she will be ready soon and make a trip to Spain. I've been to Spain and had a wonderful time. I dinnae get seasick or anything."

"Ye have been to Spain?" Hanna wondered aloud. "Ye are well-traveled for such a young girl." She wiped her hands with a rag and propped a fist at her waist. "Ye know Peigi will not like ye to stray from the castle." She leveled a pointed stare at Gillian, hoping the child did not intend to take off on her own.

Gillian hopped to the floor, a smile lighting her face. "All the more reason ye should take me to see *Alacrity* this morn. And 'tis so beautiful outside—unfair to remain cooped inside, aye?"

Hanna couldn't stop her answering smile. Gillian was so bright and engaging she could not find it in her heart to scold the child.

Frida's face floated before her, dismay contorting her features, catching Hanna off-guard. Hanna's breath stuttered.

Avenge me! Avenge us!

"Hanna?" Gillian's small voice chirped, breaking Frida's spell. Hanna startled, blinking rapidly to bring her focus to Gillian. Bjarne tilted his head, the movement widening Hanna's vision. Frida faded into the past, and Hanna forced a smile.

"Come with me, Gillian. After we finish our morning chores, we will go see this boat of yours."

* * *

Gillian skipped alongside Hanna, chattering merrily, Bjarne gamboling along behind.

"It isnae a *boat*," the child explained. "'Tis a *ship*, and 'tis the hugest ship ever—or, at least that I've seen—and I've seen some big ships," she said in all seriousness.

Hanna smothered a slight smile at Gillian's precociousness. Her heart lifted immeasurably as the child prattled away.

As they approached the harbor, Hanna's gaze rose to the tall masts on the enormous ship. Gillian grabbed her hand.

"'Tis grand, aye?" she breathed, her eyes glowing. Dread took up a slow beat in Hanna's belly.

They came in three large ships, crowded with men who wished to spill Viking blood.

"I want to go aboard," Gillian said firmly, slipping her palm from Hanna's grasp.

Hanna startled, glancing up as Gillian darted to the planks spanning the chasm between the ship and the dock.

"Gillian, wait!" she called. Picking up her skirts, Hanna hurried after the child, nearly tripping over the gangly pup that drew to a halt at the dock's edge. Eying the planks with mistrust, Bjarne crouched low, whining as Gillian continued up the walkway.

"Ahoy, *Alacrity*!" Gillian called, pausing at the edge of the ship.

"Ahoy, the dock!" a voice responded, rising above the raucous noises of shipbuilding.

"Permission to come aboard?" Gillian trilled.

"Permission granted."

Gillian cast an eager look over her shoulder. "Come on, Hanna!"

Stepping around the puppy, Hanna scurried across the plank, Gillian maintaining a steady lead. As exasperation set in and Hanna bit back scolding words, a man approached Gillian, his burly form topped by a dark auburn mane and a bushy beard to match. Hanna's heart stopped.

It cannot be! She shook her head to dispel the memory. *It is not him.* His build was the same as the leader of the men who had destroyed her family, her life. But she had met many of similar stature in the weeks since, and this man was no different from them. 'Twas only the added reminder of the ship that brought the brute to mind.

His easy smile as he glanced past Gillian reassured her somewhat. Surely the devil did not smile at children.

"I see ye have yer nurse with ye," he commented.

"This is Hanna. She's my friend. My nurse, Peigi, isnae well,"

Gillian replied.

The man's eyes narrowed against the sun. "Och, 'tis honored I am to have such bonny lasses aboard," he said. "I will alert yer da when the *Alacrity* is ready for her maiden voyage, and mayhap he will bring ye and yer friend with him." He sent Hanna a wink. "I'm needing a lassie who eats her carrots to help at the wheel that day." He chucked her under her chin, his grin wide.

"I will do my best," Gillian muttered, slanting a glance at Hanna as though hoping she hadn't heard the exchange. Her gaze strayed past Hanna. Her body stiffened and she grasped Hanna's hand tight in alarm.

"Bjarne! No!"

Too quick for Hanna to react, Gillian darted past, her screams rising in Hanna's ears. A cloud rushed before the sun, darkening the sky, and the wind increased, blowing strands of Hanna's hair into her face. Reality bent and she again heard the cries of the women—of anger and anguish and fear.

Gulls shrieked overhead. *Avenge us, Hanna!*

Hanna shook her head, but Frida's face mocked her. *Ye are not a true warrior. Ye care more for the child of our enemy than for the children you lost.*

"No!" Hanna shouted. *She is not the enemy!*

"Hanna!"

Gillian's shrill cry split the air, snapping Hanna from her anguish. She spied Gillian on her belly, sprawled across the planks on the dock. A moment's hesitation seized Hanna, but she grabbed her skirt and fled to Gillian's side.

"He fell!" Gillian sobbed, stretching her hand as far as she could toward the pup floundering in the water. She wiggled her fingers, but the reach was too far.

Hanna knelt beside her. "Gillian, let me try," she said, her voice firm, trying not to reflect the panic inside as the gentle sway of the ship created waves that swept rhythmically over Bjarne's head.

"Help him!" Gillian sobbed, scooting back a few inches to give Hanna room. "Help!"

Ignoring shouts from the ship, Hanna lay flat on the boards and reached for the pup. His yelps became less frequent as he struggled to stay afloat.

"Help!" Gillian cried again as a strong wave shoved Bjarne against a piling. She lunged forward, sliding on the wet planks. Feet pounded the boards as men responded to Gillian's cries. Rolling awkwardly from her prone position, Hanna grabbed for the back of Gillian's gown—and missed.

"Gillian!" a man's voice shouted.

Let her go! No one saved your daughter. Why should ye save the child of a Scot?

Chapter Thirteen

Alex looked up from the accounting on his desk. A young woman stood in the doorway to his solar, wringing her hands and clearly upset. He set his quill into the inkstand and rose.

"May I be of help?"

The woman glanced over her shoulder as though afraid someone would overhear. Alex motioned her inside the room. She took two steps forward then halted.

"My laird, I am Agnes," she lifted worried eyes to his. "From the kitchen."

Alex nodded. "Go on."

"I . . . I have seen the new Norsewoman with yer daughter."

Alex narrowed his eyes. "Aye. Gillian likes her."

Agnes took another step forward. "The lass has been misled. I fear she is in great danger!"

It isnae possible. Cold fear washed over him. *Hanna cannae mean to harm her. The kitchen wench is wrong.*

He tore through the castle gates, faintly aware of the soldiers who closed behind him. His feet pounded the familiar path through the village to the dock as a cry lifted on the air.

"Help!"

Torn between the need to retch and the urge to run faster, Alex clenched his fists and found a bit more speed. He crested a small hill, the view of the dock sprawled before him.

Why is Gillian fleeing the Alacrity? Who does she flee? Why does Hanna not stop her?

Gillian slipped, fell. *Where the hell is Hanna?*

Alex tore his gaze from his daughter and caught sight of the

Norsewoman as she ran from the *Alacrity* to the dock where Gillian lay.

A dip in the path cost Alex his view.

"Gillian!" Alex shouted as he raced for the dock. The soldiers in his personal guard pounded the boards behind him. Alex shoved past sailors and deck hands and sprinted up the pier. The men moved hastily aside as he charged through their ranks.

A flash of brown skirts marked Hanna's form sprawled along the dock. Gillian was nowhere to be seen, her cries muffled.

Alex's hand grabbed the hilt of his sword, the other reached forward, encountering empty air, too far away to be of help.

Let her go! The words leapt to his brain, but foundered on his lips. Did Hanna grab Gillian to help? Or did she hold the lass in the water?

"Gillian!" he roared.

With a twist of her body, Hanna rolled Gillian to the edge of the dock, clutching her to her chest. Alex reached her side and snatched Gillian away, shoving her to her feet behind him. Hanna rose to her feet, staring into the water. Men surrounded Alex and he turned his attention to Gillian, crouching at her side as he inspected every inch.

"Look, Da!" Gillian cried, struggling in his grasp. He glanced up as two men dashed after Hanna who had taken the opportunity to hurry away.

"Dinnae let her escape!" One of the men shouted. "She tried to kill the laird's bairn!"

Hanna glanced over her shoulder, her face pale. Her step faltered, and two men were on her in an instant, one on either side. Dropping her weight unexpectedly, Hanna slipped from their grasp, bringing them up short as she produced a dagger from her sleeve.

"Halt!" Alex cried.

"No!" Gillian shrieked.

Alex gripped his daughter's shoulder, passing her back to one of his soldiers. "Stay here," he commanded. Gillian scowled, a look of fierce rebellion on her face. "Dinnae disobey," Alex warned. Gillian shrugged off his hands and darted away. With a curse, Alex sprang after her, only to pull up short as Gillian pounced on Bjarne as he struggled from the loch, clutching his bedraggled form to her chest. He turned to Hanna, his heart beating erratically.

"I would hear from ye what happened."

Bright spots appeared in Hanna's cheeks. "Call off yer men," she countered. Alex nodded and the two men dropped several steps away.

"Put away yer dagger," he said. Hanna sent him a defiant look.

After a moment, she sheathed the dagger.

"I did not harm your daughter."

"Tell me what happened," he invited.

"We spoke with the captain," she nodded at the master shipbuilder, misnaming him, but Alex did not comment on her error. "He returned to his work and Gillian saw her puppy try to leap from the dock to the ship."

"He dinnae like the planks," Gillian called. "He fell in the water!"

Hanna nodded. "Gillian ran ahead of me. I . . . I should not have let her get away from me. And when I caught up with her, I grabbed for her and missed."

One of the men grumbled and shifted his feet. Hanna met his accusing glare. He took a step forward, his chest thrust out, belligerence in his eyes.

"Ye shoved her! I saw ye. The lass nearly went into the loch!"

"I caught her," Hanna replied, sending the man an arch look.

"Once we were close enough to see what ye were about," he sneered.

"I would not harm her," Hanna said.

"'Tis said ye seek revenge." The man bristled as he stalked her. "And we'll all be hanged before we allow ye to harm the bairn!"

Wind whistled in the trees, crashing waves against the shore. Bjarne whimpered in Gillian's tight grip. Alex studied the woman before him. Her eyes blazed in defiance, her dress wrapped about her in the choking grip of the coming storm. Her dagger reappeared.

"One step closer and I will pin your foot to these planks."

The man hesitated. Alex ground his jaw in frustration.

"Does the need for revenge still grip ye?" he asked. "Or are ye the woman I believe ye to be?"

Long moments passed. Tension coiled between them. "Am I wrong, Hanna?"

Hanna lifted her chin. "I saved Gillian today. Mayhap she would have merely received an unwelcome dunking had I not grabbed her. But I could not risk her being crushed between the ship and the pilings. If ye wish to believe this rabble," she nodded to the two scowling men, "'tis your privilege."

The shipmaster took a step forward. "If I may, my laird, from my viewpoint, the lady dinnae attempt to harm the bairn." He nodded at Hanna. "And it appears she harmed herself trying to save wee Gillian."

Hanna lifted fingers to her cheek where angry red streaks spoke of striking the wooden boards as she grabbed Gillian.

"Da, Hanna wouldnae hurt me. She doesnae even scold me— much." Gillian's small voice settled on Alex's heart and his apprehension melted.

"I will speak with Eric later," he said, indicating the man who'd accused Hanna. "For now, I wish to be alone with Hanna and Gillian. The rest of ye may leave."

Laird MacLean had every appearance of a patient man, but those around him vanished quickly at his dismissal. Gillian released Bjarne and moved to Hanna's side, gripping her skirts in one grubby fist as she leaned against Hanna's legs.

"Da, dinnae be angry with Bjarne. He dinnae know he couldnae leap the gap."

Angry with the dog? The laird is angry with me. Hanna wondered at Gillian's judgement.

"I am not angry with any of ye," the laird said. "Unless mayhap with the man who accused Hanna."

"He is wrong," Gillian replied matter-of-factly. "Hanna wouldnae hurt me. Hanna likes me."

The laird's gaze moved to Hanna. "Is this true?"

"I do like her," Hanna said. Her voice dropped in timbre. "And, aye, the man is wrong."

Gillian smiled happily. "Good! Scold him, Da, and he willnae do it again." She lifted her face to Hanna. "Can we go back? I'm hungry."

Hanna met the laird's gaze.

"Go back to the hall, Gillian," he said. "We will follow."

With a snap of her fingers to beckon Bjarne, Gillian skipped up the path, her troubles quickly shed. Hanna eyed the laird warily.

"Who accused me?"

He gave her a blank stare.

"Other than that man ye named Eric," she clarified. "Why did ye rush here?"

"A woman from the kitchen worried Gillian was in danger."

His prevarication irked Hanna. "A woman—and I believe I know who—turned ye against me so easily? Had I gone to your bed last night, would ye have kept a dagger beneath your pillow? Ye would bed me but not trust me?"

"I always keep a dagger," he replied. "But if I dinnae trust ye, I would have hidden it beneath the mattress." He shook his head. "Hanna, if there was no trust between us, I wouldnae invite ye to my bed. I dinnae glean added pleasure from danger. I prefer to assume I will wake with my parts intact."

Despite her cold anger at his seeming betrayal at a mere whisper from an envious source, Hanna had to suppress her smile. It would take cunning to best this man. She would not subdue him with brute strength. So far, she'd only encountered a gentle touch from him. His breadth of shoulder and corded arms promised much more.

"Hanna, I shouldnae have listened to Agnes. I am afraid where Gillian is concerned, I have a blind spot."

Hanna released a heavy breath. "I killed trying to protect my daughter," she said, her throat suddenly clogged with tears. "I will not condemn ye for wishing to protect yours."

Chapter Fourteen

Hanna lifted fingertips to her cheek, testing the salve the laird had badgered her into accepting from the healer. His concern and wry smile as he reminded her she'd suffered on behalf of his daughter, chipped away at the reserve she felt around him. It hadn't been that long ago she'd wished him great harm—perhaps even the death of his daughter.

She shivered. Not Gillian. Never Gillian. And, perhaps never the laird, either. Her desire for revenge ebbed daily, replaced by something much warmer, more wholesome. More desirable. He was a Scot, but she now knew him as a man who cared deeply, and who had treated her fairly.

He'd asked if she would accompany him after the noon meal to view the changes being made to the *Porpoise*. Part of her balked at the request to approve conditions for the Scottish king, and part of her balked at being seen so freely in the company of the MacLean laird. He'd asked her to become his mistress, and if she accompanied him, people would assume she'd accepted. That was not the role she desired.

"Are ye ready?"

Hanna glanced up as Alex poked his head through the open doorway. He seemed not at all disconcerted at being on the uppermost level of the tower, in one of the tiniest, most ill-appointed rooms in the entire castle.

"I do not think this is a good idea," she said.

He stepped fully into the doorway. "Why not?"

"I do not wish your people to get the wrong idea about me," she explained.

"They are yer people as well, for as long as ye live here," Alex protested.

"That does not change the fact that I am of an enemy clan—an enemy country. And to be seen at your side indicates a bond between us that does not exist."

"That much is true," he admitted.

"And I still must work among them," she pointed out.

"Agnes will be working in the laundry," Alex said. "Ye need not fear repercussions from her."

Hanna's eyebrows lifted.

"She chose to make trouble where none existed," Alex stated flatly. "Had ye acted in such a manner, 'twould be *ye* sortin' through the stained garments."

Justice? Impartiality? What manner of man is he?

"Will ye come? I've sent Gillian to Peigi for a nap after the morning's excitement. I dinnae wish to go alone."

"Lairds scarcely go anywhere alone," she noted drily.

He planted his feet square and crossed his arms over his chest, rooting himself firmly to the spot. "I want to go with *ye*."

"Ha! So much for not demanding my compliance," Hanna remarked, reminding him of his declaration of the night before. "Is this a condition of my stay? For ye know if I go, 'twill shorten the distance to your bed—at least in the minds of your people."

Alex grinned broadly. "Nay. I willnae put conditions on yer stay. However, I will use whatever charms are at my disposal to lure ye to my side."

"Charms?" Hanna drawled, an eyebrow cocked warily. "Filling up my doorway like a Norse god?"

He cocked his head, considering the image—the conceited man. "I dinnae believe I have ever been likened to a Norse god before," he mused. "Then again, I have never before listened to the opinions of a beautiful Norsewoman before, either."

"The women here do not praise ye?" Hanna asked, baiting him, ignoring the flutter in her belly as he named her beautiful. 'Twas a man's ploy. She knew she was not beautiful.

"I dinnae pay attention. To those of my hall, I am their laird. The women who are paraded before me as likely wife candidates mouth empty flattery. If ye refer to those who share my bed, I dinnae repeat those confidences."

Kitchen gossip came to Hanna's mind. "I have heard ye and your late wife were not often in accord," she ventured, an eye to his features, curious to see how he would react.

His smile lost position to a scowl, but he merely shook his head. "Even two years after her death the gossip doesnae cease. Mayhap ye have ample cause to balk at my request this day. I willnae demand it of ye."

Even as he released her from his request, his eyes begged her to join him. Hanna sighed. "I will put a cloak over my gown and go with ye." She indicated the stains that blotched the wool.

Alex frowned. "Do ye not have another gown?"

"Nae." Hanna hesitated. "I did not believe I would need another."

* * *

Not need another? An inconceivable thought considering his late wife's vast wardrobe. Realization dawned. "Ye knew ye would die if ye took yer revenge."

Hanna met his gaze evenly. "Aye."

Alex studied her intently. "Will ye need another gown, Hanna?"

"Aye. I believe I will."

With a nod and small sigh of relief, Alex latched on to her earlier statement. "Ye will go with me this day?"

"Lord help me, for I find it difficult to resist such an earnest plea." She reached for the cloak hanging from a peg by the door—a garment clearly at its end of use. Alex beat her to it. Handling it as though it were of finest silk, he draped it over her shoulders.

"Do not put up the hood," he said as she reached for the covering. She sent him a questioning look. "I like yer hair."

He motioned for her to precede him, hiding his smile at her startled looks. He rather enjoyed besting Hanna, provoking her into telling him her private thoughts, listening to her candor. And he enjoyed when she bested him, as well.

They stepped into the bailey, eying the dark clouds overhead.

"Do we risk a drenching, my laird?" she asked.

"If ye get so much as a drop on ye, I will have three gowns made to replace this one," Alex vowed, liking the slightly skeptical look on Hanna's face. "I can stand the cost, Hanna, but only if ye call me Alex."

His prompt hit home. Her cheeks pinked becomingly, and her glance darted away.

"Is it too difficult for ye—or should I teach it to ye in Norse?"

Her startled look returned. "What is your name—in Norse?"

"Alex."

This time his laugh could not be contained at the pained look she sent him. Placing a palm at the small of her back, he urged her across the yard. Six of his personal guard flanked them at a discreet distance. Hanna peered over her shoulder.

"So many?"

Alex followed her glance, the familiarity of his guard so ingrained, he had scarcely noticed them. "'Tis protocol," he shrugged. "Inside the walls there are usually two suitably placed to watch my back or guard whatever room I am in. Outside, there are more." He paused. "Gillian has a guard as well, though she often slips past. Since she doesnae leave the castle walls without escort, she is typically left to Peigi's watchful eye. Should she leave, she must be guarded."

He frowned. "She didnae have a guard today."

Hanna shook her head. "Nay. I am not used to such precautions."

"She would make an excellent target for ransom. Ye must promise to collect at least two soldiers to guard her should she beguile ye into taking her beyond the walls again."

"I see the danger. I will do as ye ask."

Alex held her elbow, lending support over a bit of rocky terrain. Not that he considered her fragile or incapable of comporting herself over the slight obstacle, but because he enjoyed touching her.

He sent a salute to the master shipbuilder who left his work on the *Alacrity* to join them. He fell into step as they traveled the length of the dock to the smaller ship.

"How goes the refitting?" Alex asked.

The shipmaster gave Hanna a brief bow then turned the talk to details and questions about the *Porpoise*.

"It doesnae need to be lavish," Alex reminded him. "Merely accommodating should the king decide to sail with us. Should he wish a personal flagship, I am certain we can entertain the idea at a later date."

"Then all will be in place next week. Come see for yerself."

"Excellent. We will need to sail by the end of the sennight to meet with the king."

The shipmaster beckoned them aboard. Alex assisted Hanna up the steep plank. She slipped her hand from his arm and nodded for him to proceed without her. Alex listened with half an ear to the shipmaster's comments, his eyes taking in the polished wood and metal gleaming on every inch of the ship. The captain's quarters had been enlarged and fitted with a bed, desk and chair amid ample space, and draped with heavy fabric to keep the cold air at bay. A second cabin, generally set aside for a guest—should they have a paying customer—had been similarly outfitted. A storeroom had been converted into extra sleeping quarters for soldiers, for the king would have his own, and Alex had every suspicion King Alexander would be eager to test the *Porpoise* for himself.

"I am well-pleased," Alex said. "Ye have done as I asked, and in a timely manner. My thanks."

The shipmaster gave a deep nod of acceptance of the compliments. Duty performed, Alex was instantly diverted.

"I will ensure the foodstuffs and anything else ye need are available." He spun about, seeking Hanna.

She lingered not far from where he'd left her, her gaze traveling the distant horizon.

"What captures yer thoughts, Hanna?" he asked.

"They came in the night—three black ships lit by lanterns and torches."

Alex gingerly wrapped his arms about her, feeling the fine shiver that wracked her body. Mayhap he had won her trust. It would take time to conquer her demons.

Chapter Fifteen

It wasn't that Alex was starving, he'd simply never been able to resist the aroma of fresh-baked pasties. And, as laird, it was less likely he'd get his hands slapped for sneaking a hot pie from the cooling table. His belly grumbled as he shucked out of his sweat-stained leine. This morning's sword practice had been grueling, and he'd lingered amid the well-trained group of much younger men for no other reason than he did not look forward to an afternoon of bookkeeping.

Alex quickly sluiced water over his neck and shoulders and reached for a rough scrap of linen to dry with, deciding to grab a couple of Cook's prized pies before settling in at his desk. The growing aroma seemed destined to drive him to distraction.

He scrubbed his thick hair and draped the cloth over his shoulders, certain he would require a clean leine before resuming his duties, and hesitant to let the pies cool before he returned to collect one.

"Which would ye prefer first?" The feminine, matter-of-fact voice startled him. Alex slewed his head around, his gaze landing on Hanna's slim form standing patiently to one side. He feasted a moment on her brow arched over dark green eyes, her mouth not quite lifting into a smile. One of her hands held a folded—and presumably clean—leine, the other, a small platter boasting two steaming pasties.

"Ye have lived here little more than a month, and ye know me so well?" Alex asked, his stomach rumbling at the sight of the pies, though his cock stirred with a different hunger.

"Ye arenae a difficult man to understand, my laird," Hanna replied, lifting first one hand then the other, asking him to choose. "And your daughter has already made her choice." With a grin, Alex snagged a pie, managing to devour it in two large bites as he sucked cool air over his teeth to ease the burn of the hot treat.

Patient, Hanna waited until his hands were free, then offered the shirt with a pointed look at his half-dressed state. Alex sucked a bit of escaped fruit from the edge of his palm, then snatched the leine and pulled it over his head, grumbling silently that he would not have asked her to cover herself had the tables been turned. He jerked the hem past his hips, surreptitiously adjusting the fit of his trews.

Grabbing the second pie, he ate it slowly, savoring the flavors as Hanna set the empty platter aside and stepped close to tie the strings at his neck. Her scent drifted to him, challenging the lure of the pasties. He silenced the groan in his chest, fighting the urge to press against her. He wondered briefly what she would do if he hiked up her skirts and backed her against the wall of the keep, her legs about his waist.

With a pat to the bow, she turned to collect her platter.

Disgruntled with the end of his fantasies, he shoved the last of the pasty in his mouth.

"'Ows Gi'lan?" he asked.

Hanna glanced over her shoulder. She then faced him, both hands on the rim of the platter as she held it flat against her skirt.

"She is a charming child," Hanna said. "Though I wonder if she would benefit from a tutor. Someone who spoke as many languages as she does." This time one edge of her lips lifted, casting the hint of a smile in her eyes.

Alex swallowed, intrigued by the sight. "Ye appear to be well," he murmured.

A faint blush tinted her cheeks. "I suppose the correct reply is *thank ye*, as I will assume that was an honest statement, not a leer and suggestion of behavior I have already declined."

"St. Andrew's toenails, lass!" Alex exclaimed, not so much surprised as disgruntled to force his ardor aside once again. "Ye are free to live here without conditions—have I not stated that enough? Though ye are also free to assume I willnae refuse a small kiss of gratitude should ye be so inclined."

Hanna's eyebrow lifted. "My *inclination* is to not rush headlong into something I am not ready for. I am too recently a widow, as ye well know."

"Tell me of him," Alex urged, unaccountably jealous of the man who'd commanded Hanna's body, her loyalty—her touch.

"Why would ye wish to know of him?" Hanna asked, her expression guarded.

"Because it tells me more of ye."

Hanna stared at him for a moment, then shrugged. "Torvald and I married to unite two clans by blood," she said, indulging his curiosity. "He was a good leader and a good father."

"Was he a good husband?"

Hanna's gaze narrowed as though unwilling to speak ill of the dead. "He kept food on the table and discipline in our home."

"Did ye love him, Hanna?"

"I did not dislike him. He was honorable and clearly loved our children."

Alex absorbed the dry facts. "Ye already know my wife and I endured a largely loveless marriage. Mayhap we tried too hard in the beginning. Our clans had been bitter enemies and we dared not fail." Alex sighed. "But the loss of the twins, and our son soon after, ended what tenuous relationship we had. Gillian was born much later and was a bit of a surprise to her ma and me."

"Still, ye must miss her."

Alex considered her statement, hearing the slight question in her voice. "She was not a difficult woman, and my marriage could have been far worse. Yet, I feel as though I've missed out on something."

Hanna's lips parted slightly, as though she wished to say more, then changed her mind.

"My sister's marriage began as one of convenience," Alex continued. "But they developed a passion for each other rarely seen. I dinnae remember my own mother—she died when I was a bairn—but everyone always said she and my da loved each other greatly. My da missed out on many years of marriage—but he dinnae miss out on love."

* * *

Hanna returned to the kitchen, taking her time as she mused over Alex's statement. Had she missed out on love? Almost certainly she had from her husband, for though he'd been a lusty man, he'd been considerate enough to never force her, and he'd always finished quickly. There had been a few times, howbeit . . .. No, better to not think of such things. Torvald was dead. It was too soon to consider another alliance—certainly not to a Scot! As long as she remained apart from her people, marriage was beyond her reach.

But was love?

Hanna crossed the kitchen, gave the platter a quick rinse and set it aside to dry. Heading out the door to the kennel where she'd left Gillian pestering the kennel master for tricks she could teach Bjarne, she caught sight of Laird MacLean filching another of Cook's pasties, though he bent forward and kissed the woman's proffered cheek as she waved a wooden spoon around his head in implied threat. The formalities accomplished, Cook slipped a second pie onto the small plate and shooed him away. His grin lit up the kitchen, as cheerful as any lad, and he bowed before his eyes met hers.

A tingle wafted across Hanna's skin. He was manly enough to capture any woman's attention, but she despaired of joining the ranks of unattached ladies angling for more than a glimpse of the MacLean laird.

Foolishness! If she remained at MacLean Castle, there were other available men should she wish to form an attachment. Though she'd seen none to compete with Alex MacLean.

She indulged in his gaze, dark and mysterious, bold and daring. What would his kiss be like? Would his chiseled lips soften against hers? She didn't imagine they would be hard and impersonal. His casual touch sent tingles flashing across her skin. How would a caress make her feel? Her belly warmed at the thought.

Would he honor any child they might conceive?

Hanna bit her lip pensively. Would she alone bear the responsibility for their actions?

His lips lifted in a smile and he departed, carrying his platter with him—and leaving Hanna to wonder at what he offered.

She sighed. It was too soon. Torvald deserved to be remembered. And yet, had he died of natural causes, she would have been pressured into remarrying quickly to maintain the leadership of the clan. And without family or kin, who was there to council her?

Did she wish to subject herself to the authority of another man, or did she value what little liberty she had? And, if she allowed the baron's attentions, what would happen to her when Alex MacLean took another wife?

Chapter Sixteen

Arbela narrowed her gaze on her brother, puzzlement warring with pleasure at his apparent good humor. He surveyed the crowd in the hall as the people went about their tasks, a faint smile on his face—as if he anticipated something.

"What has ye in such fine spirits?" she asked.

Alex sent her a startled look. "How am I different?"

"Your smiles were sad last I saw ye, Brother," Arbela replied, giving his hair a teasing ruffle, as though he was a lad. "Ye appear to have shed worries and years since I last saw ye."

"I wasnae in my best form after Annag's funeral," Alex reminded her.

"Nae, even before that ye seemed brittle—almost harsh. I suspected it had much to do with Father's and young Donal's deaths and clan responsibilities in addition to the trade ye oversee." Arbela dropped her voice. "And with a wife who left ye too much on your own. I do not applaud her death, but I am happy to see ye more relaxed."

A ruckus rose in the back of the hall—shrill barks and girlish laughter amid the clatter of a bench on the stone floor. Arbela cast a quick look toward her brother, expecting a scowl. But the look on his face dropped her jaw. Eyes intent on the people emerging from the disturbance, his hungry smile widened. She whipped her gaze to the back of the room and spied Gillian chattering merrily to a blonde woman at her side as they approached the head table.

The woman was not Gillian's nurse.

"Has Peigi outlived her usefulness?" she asked. Alex did not answer. Arbela thumped his shoulder for ignoring her and gave

Gillian a warm smile as the lass shrieked and bounded around the table to her side.

"How is my favorite niece?" Arbela scooped Gillian into a fierce hug.

The child laughed and returned the hug. "I am yer only niece," she retorted.

"Can't ask for better odds than that, then," Arbela teased.

"What are *odds*?" Gillian wanted to know.

"Arbela!" Alex warned.

"Could ye introduce me to yer new nurse?" Arbela asked, adroitly changing the subject.

Gillian hopped from her lap and grabbed the woman's hand, dragging her forward. "This is Hanna," she said, couching her tone in a formal manner. "Hanna, this is my Auntie Bela, Da's sister. She lives at Dunfaileas, but she lived here when she was a wee lass like me."

Hanna's wary gaze skipped from Gillian to Arbela—and at last to Alex.

"'Tis a pleasure to meet ye," Arbela replied, puzzling the look Hanna and Alex exchanged.

"The pleasure is mine, my lady," Hanna answered, returning her attention to the introduction. Though her voice was moderate, her words held a lilt Arbela had heard before.

"Norse?" she asked.

Hanna's eyes flashed. "Aye."

Arbela gave her a pleasant smile. "Ye are welcome here."

Hanna glanced again at Alex. "So I've been told."

"She's not my nurse," Gillian interrupted. "She's my friend. Peigi has been ill, and Hanna is a lot more fun. So is Aadny."

"Aadny?" Arbela asked, pinning Alex with a look.

"She and Hanna arrived the same day," he drawled. "Aadny has been like an elder sister to Gillian. Though not so bossy—or nosey." He returned Arbela's look with a raised brow.

Arbela favored his quip with a grin then turned to Gillian. "I came to see how much ye and the puppy have grown, and to see that yer da was staying out of trouble. Where is this beast I sent ye?"

"Bjarne!" Gillian called, taking several steps beyond the table as she searched for the dog. "He must have gone outside. There was a cat just inside the door. I 'spect ye heard."

"Aye. I believe we did," Arbela said. "Mayhap ye'd best go find him, and I will join ye in a bit." She nodded to Hanna. "'Twas a pleasure meeting ye. I hope we get a chance to chat before I leave."

"I look forward to it, my lady," Hanna replied before excusing herself to chase after Gillian.

Alex's gaze lingered on the Norsewoman's form as she strode away.

"So, that is who keeps ye from answering my invitations to visit?"

* * *

Mesmerized by the sway of Hanna's hips, Alex reluctantly pulled from his trance and gave his attention to Arbela, hoping to deflect her curiosity. Her grin told him she saw far more than he intended.

"Gillian is helping Hanna overcome her grief at losing her family," he said.

Arbela burst out laughing. "Such a sanctimonious tone! Ye are anxious to help her forget her past as well."

Alex drummed his fingertips on the arm of his chair. "So what if I am? The council has been after me this past year to find a woman of my choice."

"Aye, and marry her," Arbela reminded him. "Do ye intend to marry this Norsewoman?"

"The thought had crossed my mind," Alex grumbled, vexed to hear his quandary falling from her lips.

"What will the council say?"

"I care not," he replied, his ire rising.

"Ye should," Arbela pointed out. "Though ye are the MacLean, they are yer council."

"They shouldnae worry over who I take to bed," Alex groused.

"They willnae," she agreed. "But binding the clan to a woman clearly of Norse descent could put ye and the clan in a precarious position with the king."

Alex wanted to shout he was perfectly capable of managing his own clan politics, but he knew his sister merely spoke the obvious.

"Do ye not have an appointment with the king in a fortnight's time?" she pushed.

"What would ye have me do? Ask his blessing on my marriage to a Norsewoman as we plot to wrest the King of Norway's hold on the Isles?"

Arbela leaned closer, placing a hand over his. "Have ye spoken of yer wishes to Hanna?"

Alex gave a curt nod.

"How did she respond? Does she hold back from marrying ye?"

Alex frowned. Why did it seem Arbela approved the thought Hanna might have strong feelings about marrying a Scot?

"I dinnae ask her to marry me."

Arbela drew back. "Ye said ye did."

"Nay. I dinnae ask her to marry me. I asked her to become my mistress."

Arbela's chair squealed on the stone floor as she pushed forcefully to her feet. "Come with me."

Her command, unyielding from years mothering her own brood, left him little choice. He took a final sip from his cup and rose to follow. They entered his solar and Arbela slammed the door behind them.

"Have ye lost yer mind? Has auld age caught up with ye at last? My brother, the gallant knight to whom lasses tossed their virginity—"

"I never deflowered an innocent!" Alex protested. "One. I was unaware. She was verra convincing. And 'twas before I married."

Arbela poked his chest with her forefinger. "Ye spent nearly thirty married years being faithful to yer wife. And now that ye are free to marry again, ye have spent the past year plying the Mediterranean coastline, though I imagine ye have at least learned discretion."

"I dinnae swive my way through the port towns," he growled. "I had my daughter with me."

Arbela's eyebrows arched in an ironic gesture he knew too well. "Be that as it may, ye now have a woman in mind—she's very lovely, by the way, and Gillian seems smitten by her—and ye do naught but stare after her like a lovesick lad! Serves ye right she willnae do more than exchange puppy's eyes with ye. Offering to make her yer mistress! Pah!"

Alex shook his head like an ox stunned by a butcher's blow. "Are ye saying I *should* marry a Norsewoman?"

"Not *a* Norsewoman, *that* Norsewoman," Arbela corrected. "Or at least give her the courtesy of speaking yer heart to her. I can imagine the drivel ye've spilled to keep her at arm's length. Ye are quite out of the habit of wooing, Brother."

Chapter Seventeen

The laird caught Hanna's eye with a quick gesture as Arbela engaged Gillian in a conversation regarding her puppy's virtues. Hanna stepped away, answering a peculiar urge to be near him. His interest piqued her curiosity and, against her better judgement—as her heart tripped a strange, eager cadence—she joined him as he skirted a pile of badly worn wooden shields laying at the edge of the practice field.

She folded her hands within the wide cuffs of her sleeves and fell into step next to him with a glance over her shoulder to where the older woman frolicked with Gillian and her puppy.

"Och, my sister is a fine lass," Laird MacLean rumbled, "and we were always thick as thieves growing up. We're twins—can ye tell?"

Again, Hanna slanted Arbela a look from the corner of her eyes. "Ye do favor. Your eyes are different, though."

"'Tis her way," he said. "We were born and raised in the Holy Land, and our mother was Armenian. Arbela endured two cold winters here before she gave up her satins and brocades for sturdy wool, though she still has a fondness for silks and jewels, and is often seen in trews and a tunic." He grinned. "She smudges her eyes with kohl, though not as much as before."

"She is very beautiful," Hanna murmured, surprised to learn their mother had not been Scottish.

She followed him, admiring the warrior grace of his muscles, until he at last came to a halt some distance away, behind the stable where broodmares grazed, their bellies swelling with the next year's foals. Alex leaned against the stable wall, facing the peaceful scene. He caught Hanna's hand and led her to stand before him, her back against his chest.

Hanna tensed as his arms encircled her, equally startled at the thrill of his touch and fear of a trap.

"I believe I've mentioned before, should I wish to toss ye in the dungeon, I have no need of resorting to trickery. I brought ye here because I've been wanting to hold ye, and there are too many damn people around anywhere else."

Releasing her panic, Hanna settled to the warmth of his encircling arms, his breath against her cheek—and the firm evidence of his desire against her buttocks. New heat blossomed, sliding up her neck from an indescribable place deep inside.

Alex's voice rumbled. "I watch ye with Gillian and wonder what it would have been like to see ye grow round with child, to be at yer side to welcome a bairn into this world. I wonder if a child of ours would have had yer coloring or mine."

"My laird—"

"Alex," he reminded her, his lips brushing the top of her ear. Hanna swallowed.

"Alex," she breathed, "what ye ask is . . .."

"Is what?" he asked when she did not continue. "Is sordid? Dishonorable? Distasteful to ye? Or could it be passionate? Beautiful? Fulfilling?"

Hanna leaned forward, breaking from his embrace, then faced him. "I do not believe it would be distasteful to lie with ye. Though my experience of passion is lacking, I believe ye would be a generous lover." She stepped close again as he settled his hands at her waist, placing herself between his feet. Catching a whiff of his scent, she drew an indulgent breath, heady with the scent of warm wool and man.

"Hanna, I willnae force ye. But could we experiment? And if ye dinnae like it, we willnae pursue it." He tilted his head. "At least let us say we tried."

"What do ye suggest?" she asked, of two minds where her loyalties lay. How much of herself was she willing to give up to sample the enigma she found in this man?

Alex's fingertips stroked the line of her jaw. "A simple kiss, Hanna," he murmured. "We dinnae wish to scandalize the horses."

His quip brought a smile to her lips, and he was quick to capture it, slanting his mouth across hers. He nibbled her lower lip, traced it with his tongue. Sparks ignited every inch of her, challenging her senses in a way she'd never experienced. Aware of every texture and contour of his lips, she boldly answered his unspoken question, opening her mouth to receive his plundering caress, meeting his escalating ardor with a passion that took her unaware.

Alex's body, disarmingly relaxed only a moment before, tensed as he pulled her against his length. Hanna twined her arms about his neck, pressing against him as the surge of his mouth demanded her surrender. She denied his command, forcing him back as she sought more. A whimper escaped her as she met the solid wall of his chest.

She slid one knee up his thigh, opening herself to the hard caress of his cock as Alex's hand gripped her buttocks through the layers of her skirts. His groan filled her ears. He shoved the layers of fabric back and scooped her up, pivoting as he pressed Hanna's back against the wall. She wrapped her legs about his waist and surrendered to his mouth with a sigh.

Alex ground his cock against her core. Panting, he pressed his forehead against hers.

"By St. Andrew's balls," he said, his voice harsh, "what is there about passion ye dinnae understand?"

Hanna's grin spread across her swollen lips. "Ye name that a simple kiss?" she countered.

"I believe we have scandalized the horses and dashed all previous notions of mere kissing beyond recall." Alex groaned and pressed closer. "Ye cannae be unaffected."

Hanna's breath caught between a laugh and a groan, emerging as a gasp as fire lit every nerve. Overhead, thunder rumbled. Hanna blinked, suddenly aware of dark clouds where an overcast sky had been moments before. Lightning cracked and a low drone filled her ears.

Alex yelped and slid to one side, taking refuge from the rain's onslaught beside her beneath the stable roof's overhang. He found her hand and gripped it as though he feared she would flee. He kissed the top of her head.

"I have an idea. Follow me."

* * *

The fragrant scent of fresh hay filled his nose. Cut ends of the dry grass poked at him through the plaide crumpled beneath him in places that hadn't been poked in many years. What had possessed him to seduce Hanna in the stable loft?

Finish seducing Hanna was perhaps a better phrase. Or, had she seduced him? He was certain he'd never experienced anything quite like his Valkyrie. Hanna curled against him, sound asleep, likely exhausted from a bout of lovemaking that left him wondering when he'd be able to move again.

The hay crackled softly as he rolled his head from side to side and stretched his legs. Hanna sighed and slid a hand across his chest, anchoring him in place.

The driving sound of rain eased and Alex heard the rattle of buckets and murmur of voices below, marking the evening feeding. His stomach ventured a growl, but it lacked conviction.

Hanna of Hällstein, what have ye done to me?

With an effort, he rolled to his side and pressed a kiss to Hanna's forehead. A slightly salty flavor tingled on his lips.

"We could stay the night, but I believe we'd be more comfortable in my bed," he whispered.

Hanna's eyes flew open, the line of her body tensed. Before calming words left his mouth, she eased. Hay rustled as she tilted her head slightly. "Ye wish to continue this?" she asked.

"I hoped this was not a single event," Alex drawled as his cock stirred to life at the sound of her voice. "I admit the experience met my most hearty approval. What say ye, Hanna? Will ye have me?"

Hanna's hand returned to stroke his chest, her fingers twisting gently in the mat of hair. "'Twas more than I expected," she admitted. "I did not know men and women could enjoy this together."

Jealousy roiled in Alex's gut. "Yer husband dinnae care for yer affections?"

Hanna shook her head. "He came to me often—and finished quickly."

"I would show ye generosity in love, Hanna. If ye but give me a chance."

"Ye already have," she replied. "I regret not one moment in your arms."

Alex narrowed his eyes, a frown playing about his lips. "Ye dinnae sound certain ye wish to add to those moments," he said. "If ye have no regrets, then what is it ye fear?"

Hanna was silent for a moment, then rose from their make-shift bed, settling on the blanket with her legs tucked beneath her. She trapped her hands between her knees, giving him a frank look, though Alex thought he saw a flash of sorrow lurking in the dark green depths. His gaze dropped lower, admiring the play of shadowy afternoon light on her pale breasts, and the smooth curve of her hips. He clenched his hands into fists and forced himself to listen.

"I fear stepping aside when ye take a Scottish lass for a wife."

Alex risked cupping her chin in his palm. His pulse raced as skin touched skin and he wanted her again with the fervor of a youth. "I dinnae plan to take a wife," he said. "I can name Gillian my heir, or, if the council is against it, my sister's son who fostered here as a youth would make an admirable laird. Ye and I are free to enjoy each other for as long as we wish."

Hanna shook her head, her skin soft beneath his touch. "I was raised to be a shield maiden, not a temptress."

"Ye are a strong woman," Alex agreed. He ran his thumb over the ridge of her cheek bone. "But ye were meant to stand with a man, not oppose him."

"Alex, there will come a time when ye will wed—for an heir, an alliance, mayhap even for love. But it willnae be me, and it would break my heart to walk away."

"Then marry me," Alex demanded. "I have no use for vows to bind me to the woman I love. But if it makes a difference to ye, I will proclaim before God and the MacLeans that ye are my wife until death parts us."

Hanna sighed. "I will not be accepted. Our people are at war. Your king readies to overthrow the King of Norway." She reached for her chemise. "When we enter the hall, we will be laird and servant once more."

"Dinnae pull away, Hanna." Alex seized the soft gown before she could slip it over her head. "A woman who fears loss, loves much. Do ye love me?"

"I cannot account for it," Hanna replied. "Ye are a Scot, and I had no knowledge of ye little more than a month ago. But I find much to admire in ye."

"That isnae what I asked," Alex growled. "Do ye love me?"

Hanna glanced downward, as though she could see through the hay and rafters to the stable below. "In half an hour, the stable hands will be at their supper and we can slip away unseen." She slid a hand up his arm and across his shoulder, trailing her fingertips down his chest and belly to where his cock awaited her.

"Let me show ye the answer."

Chapter Eighteen

Arbela glanced up from tightening her horse's girth and sent her brother a sharp look. "I thought ye would be in a better mood to see me off."

"She doesnae want me."

Arbela snorted. "She wanted ye very badly, if ye ask me. Did ye offer to marry her?"

"Aye."

"And the offer fell flat after ye sought her as yer mistress." Arbela's statement hit too close and Alex glared at her. She shrugged. "Even as desirable as ye must be—and dinnae look to me for praise. Ye are my brother, after all, and I know yer secrets. Even so, a woman who loves with her heart doesnae wish to be counted as secondary in yer life."

"And being a wife doesnae place her first?"

Arbela lifted an eyebrow. "Ye arenae so daft as to believe a bride is instantly elevated to such a status once the ink is dry on the contract. 'Tis a rare relationship that gives husband and wife equal footing." She gave the girth a sharp tug then tightened the knot and dropped the stirrup leather.

"Ye've dug yerself quite a hole, Brother. I wish ye all the best, and I would be happy to claim Hanna as my sister by marriage. But if ye wish to keep her, ye must give her more than a memorable tupping. Ye must give her yer heart."

Arbela swung into the saddle and gathered her reins. The mounted guard came to attention. "*Gnas barov*, Alex. I hope to see ye in a better mood next I visit."

Arbela and her armed escort clattered from the yard, the horses' hooves flinging up bits of damp earth. Alex peered at the sky, calculating the possibility of an hour's time to check on the *Porpoise* before they set sail two days hence. Sailing was something he knew, and knew well—a comforting thought among a host of disquieting ones.

After their time together the day before, Alex knew Hanna's body, though not nearly as well as he'd like, and his body craved hers like nothing he'd ever known before. If he couldn't win her heart and convince her to accept his proposal before he sailed, he wondered if he'd get another chance.

* * *

Gillian bounced up and down in Aadny's lap, her squeal of indignation echoing in the small chamber. Restless at being cooped up in the castle as rain settled in again after the evening meal, Gillian had demanded a story. Hanna and Aadny's room beneath the eaves proved the perfect place to avoid Peigi whose aching bones shortened her patience—and for Hanna to finally relax her vigil against meeting with Alex again. The effect he'd had on her senses had both thrilled and disquieted her, sharpening her reaction to the least sound or movement. She did not want to need him so badly. 'Twas foolishness to believe he had done little more than appease a need, a curiosity. Twice she'd wondered if she would be better off leaving the sanctuary of MacLean Castle. If not for Aadny and Gillian, she would have done more than consider the unsettling thought.

"Och! They killed Thjadi?" Gillian wrinkled her nose. "They burnt him up?"

Hanna tilted her head, trying to remember which story she'd recited. Ah, Loki and the giant.

"The giant *had* been chasing Loki," she explained. "'Twas all the gods could do to protect him—and themselves. The gods were thankful Loki had brought Idun back, for they were aging, and only she could keep them young."

Gillian considered this, then nodded. "And all was well once Idun returned?"

Hanna met Aadny's gaze. "Not entirely," she admitted. "For when Thjadi died, his daughter, Skadi, showed up in the middle of their celebration to avenge her father's death."

Irony poked at Hanna for telling Gillian a story involving revenge when it had been the master of her heart for so long. A peculiar sense of well-being crept over her as she gazed at the child and the young girl she'd taken under her wing. A smile teased one corner of her mouth.

"What happened?" Gillian asked, eager for the rest of the story.

"Well, 'twas not easy to convince Skadi to put aside her vengeance, but the gods were patient with her and she eventually agreed to terms of reparation."

"What is re-par-shun?" Gillian puzzled.

"Reparation is terms to repay you for a wrong done to you."

Gillian's eyes grew wide. "What did they give her?"

"Three things," Hanna replied. "First, the gods took Thjadi's eyes and cast them into the sky, where they became two bright stars."

Gillian frowned, then her face cleared. "I suppose that is pretty," she admitted.

"It sounds gruesome, but somehow lovely, and mayhap an honor," Hanna agreed. "A way to remember Thjadi every time you peer at the night sky."

Gillian clapped her hands, her good humor returned. "My ma looks down from the sky at me, so that was a good gift. What else did they give her?"

"The second boon was to make her laugh. Skadi was much too solemn and sad, and the gods swore they'd make her laugh." Hanna affected a woeful face. "But though the gods tried many things, none were successful in making Skadi laugh—or even smile."

"Och, no!" Gillian exclaimed in dismay. "Did that make her angry?"

"It may have," Hanna replied. "But Loki, whose name means *trickster*, tied one end of a rope about a goat's neck and . . .." Her gaze flew to Aadny's who instantly closed her eyes, pinching her mouth closed against her laughter. "And he began a game of tug of war with the goat," she finished lamely, certain the image of Loki tying one end of the rope around the goat's neck and the other about *his own testicles* would only bring confusion to the story—and perhaps uncomfortable questions from the six-year-old.

Gillian's brow drew downward. "And that made her laugh?"

"Aye," Aadny choked. "It did."

Gillian sighed as if the Norse logic escaped her, but she accepted the story. "What was her third boon?"

"Marriage to the god of her choice," Hanna said. "However, she had to choose her husband by the sight of his legs only."

"My da has bonny legs," Gillian announced. "All the women say so."

"Listening to talk ye shouldn't?" Hanna asked, giving the child a mock-severe look, attempting to pull her mind from the memory of Alex's muscular legs twined with hers.

Gillian shrugged. "Adults dinnae always remember I'm there. Did Skadi chose the right pair of legs?"

Observant child. "No. She sought the pair she believed belonged to Baldur, a god who was beloved by everyone, and quite handsome as well. The legs she chose turned out to be Njord's."

"Was that bad?" Gillian asked, leaning against Aadny for

comfort, a worried look on her face.

Hanna shrugged one shoulder. "He was a very wealthy sea god, but the problem between them was they neither one could bear living at the other's home. Njord loved the sea and the cry of gulls, and Skadi cherished the snow-covered mountains and the howl of wolves on the air. They soon parted ways and were never together again."

Gillian frowned. "My da is supposed to marry again because he needs a lad to be laird when he is gone. I want him to be happy." Her chin thrust forward in resolute decision. "I will see he doesnae choose a wife because of her legs!"

She paused, worrying her lip with her two front teeth. "Did ye live near the sea, Hanna?"

"Yes," Hanna replied. "Why?"

"Was it verra different there? Do ye like it here?"

"I am content here, *skatten min*," Hanna said. "Ye and Aadny have filled a hole in my heart and replaced a dark place with much light."

Gillian nodded solemnly. "It was like that when my ma died. My da and I went away for a year because he was too sad to stay here. I am glad ye are here, Hanna. Aadny and I will take care of ye." She cocked her head. "Mayhap Da will help."

Hanna nearly choked. Gillian's da's *help* had tossed her into a torment of indecision. Why hadn't she known giving in to the urge to bed the MacLean laird was a bad idea? Because she'd had no experience with what he called making love. Submitting quietly to Torvald resembled making love with Alex as much as dangling her feet in a placid loch resembled braving a storm-tossed sea. Succumbing to the lure of his touch had left her sated yet hungering for more.

Help? I daresay I need help. But not from your beautiful father, skatten min. No, I would not survive his eventual dismissal. I will not allow him to break my heart.

Chapter Nineteen

A summons to the Laird's solar the next day sent conflicting waves of anticipation and dread through Hanna, quickening her pulse. Alex's intense looks as she went about her daily duties in the hall let her know he hadn't forgotten their stolen time in the stable loft and wasn't about to give up seeking to further their relationship. She squared her shoulders and rapped on the closed door.

Wariness building, she waited for his command to enter, but none came. Exasperated at the wasted time, she took a half-step away, then, after a moment's hesitation, grasped the latch and opened the door. Alex was not in the room, but a large bundle rested in prominence on his desk. A piece of parchment lay atop the packet, drawing Hanna's curiosity.

She stepped to the desk, surprise widening her eyes as she read the single word on the strip of parchment, the print in a bold, masculine hand.

Hanna.

She touched the close-woven cloth bundle, her fingertips scarcely registering the weave of the wool before she drew back. The door snicked shut behind her and she whirled as though caught in a treacherous act.

Alex strode across the room his head tilted in a gesture of curiosity.

"Do ye like it?"

"Like it?" Hanna's eyes narrowed. What exactly did he ask? His question set alarms skittering beneath her skin. Did she like their stolen moments? The feel of his skin beneath her fingers? His dark hair and almond-shaped eyes? Eyes she now knew were a legacy from his Armenian mother. His offer to share his bed? Of marriage? Her certainty neither would work soured the pang of longing rippling in counterpoint to the wariness. She scowled.

"I have thought ye many things, Hanna," Alex said as he perched one hip on the edge of the desk and folded his hands in his lap. "But being illiterate isnae one of them." He nodded to the bundle. "'Tis yers."

His bold assessment heightened her simmering resentment. "It has my name written upon it but naught else. Deviousness isnae one of your vices—that I know of."

"Ye wound me," he reproached. "I have no desire to hurt ye or cause ye to distrust me. Would ye do me the honor of opening the bundle and accepting it as the gift it is?"

Her reproach deflated slightly and a tiny thrill shot through her. A gift? Her curiosity threatened to become a smile at the unexpected offer.

Alex tilted his head at the packet and Hanna touched it again, then slowly pulled it to the edge of the desk. She deftly untied the plaid ribbon, the wool so fine it slid like velvet through her fingers. Unfolding the cloth revealed a pelt of incredible plushness that invited her caress. At Alex's encouraging nod, she picked it up. The fur edged a long cloak of deep russet, the weave thick yet supple, guaranteeing warmth and comfort.

"Put it on," Alex urged.

Hanna glanced at him. His dark eyes glittered, pleasure tilting the corners of his mouth.

"I cannot accept such a gift," she murmured.

"Why not? 'Tis mine to give. There are no conditions if ye accept." His mouth hardened into a straight line. "Ye know I want ye. Ye also know I have sworn the choice is yers. Can ye not accept that it pleases me to please ye?"

A whisper of feminine delight warred with the boundary she'd sworn to place between them. "It places me in your debt," she replied, realizing how churlish she sounded. "I would think of ye every time I wore it."

Her confession restored a tiny bit of Alex's humor. "There is naught wrong with that. As long as thinking of me brings ye happiness."

He stood, angling his body close to hers. Picking up the cloak, he draped it about her shoulders. "I dinnae believe ye will need this until the cold months approach. Mayhap by then ye will have decided to accept my offer."

Placing a kiss to her temple, he took a step back, nodding as he perused her. "The cloak was made for ye and none other. It looks beautiful on ye. Keep it."

His boots thumped the stone floor as he left the room. Hanna fingered the soft wool and rubbed her cheek against the plush collar. But the warmth inside spiraled from the spot on her face where the touch of his lips lingered.

* * *

The bedtime story had become a nightly ritual, but this night, Gillian's questions put aside tales of monsters and intrigue, insisting on knowing more of Aadny's family.

"I was separated from them many months ago," Aadny tried to explain, but Gillian cocked her head in puzzlement.

"I s'pose my da could have lost me in Spain, but he and Peigi dinnae let me out of their sight. Did ye wander off?"

Aadny's lips thinned, though she did not appear angry at Gillian's question.

"Nay. I escaped. Men had come to raid my village, and I slipped away before I could be captured."

Hanna shook her head. It was a tale too common and too heart-breaking.

Aadny sent Hanna a worshipful look. "And Hanna saved me from men on the docks a few days after I arrived here. I am very grateful to have met her."

"Och, I am glad I met her, also," Gillian asserted. "She is a braw woman—and my da likes ye." Her chin tilted as she slanted her gaze to Hanna. One of Hanna's eyebrows shot upward.

"I asked him long ago if he wanted another wife—after Ma died, ye know. And he said we'd pick one out together." She beamed. "Now I have ye!"

Aadny giggled and Gillian joined in. Hanna did not. "I do not think your da needs a Norsewoman for a wife."

"Och, he doesnae care what the council says," Gillian said matter-of-factly. "And I dinnae wish a ma who is young and pretty."

"But ye approve of *me*?" Hanna asked, one side of her mouth tilted in irony.

"Aye. Ye are verra brave and strong—my da says so. I know that is important to him, because my Auntie Bela is verra brave." Gillian sent Hanna an assessing look. "Ye are beautiful—not like the others. They are silly and false."

A slight ache started in Hanna's temple. The child was determined to make a match and Hanna wondered if Alex had anything to do with it.

"The servants say the laird is a just man," Aadny chimed in. "And he has a fine form." Her eyes twinkled, refusing Hanna's silent rebuke.

Gillian grinned. "My da is verra kind and everyone loves him," she put forth, possibly with a bit too much emphasis on the kindness and love. Hanna remembered the harsh man who had not blinked an eye as she stood over the man she'd killed on the dock, blood liberally marking her guilt. Instead of imprisoning her as was his right, he'd had the other miscreants hanged. And Agnes served in the laundry, though he'd warned Hanna that she would have suffered the same fate had she lied to him. *Just?* Yes. *Kind?* No.

And yet, she'd seen him with his daughter. A firm hand that bespoke abundant love for the wee one. She'd seen him kiss the top of Gillian's head and tickle her toes, give her a puppy and steal her berry pasties.

Hanna stood abruptly. "I believe we should all get some sleep." She grabbed the blanket from the foot of Gillian's bed and shook it out.

Gillian frowned as she slid prone and plopped her head on the feather-stuffed pillow. "Do ye not like talking about my da?"

"I believe your da is a fine man," Hanna prevaricated, ignoring Aadny's look of interest. "Ye should not meddle in adult business." She patted the blanket about Gillian, tucking it close against her.

With a sigh, Gillian closed her eyes. "Someone should," she murmured.

"Go to sleep, Gillian," Hanna reproved.

"He would make a good husband," Gillian insisted.

Hanna dropped a quick kiss on the child's forehead. Gillian's eyes flashed open.

"And ye would be a good ma."

* * *

Hanna set the tray on the table, giving it a quick wipe to discourage mice. The tabby cat on the banked hearth blinked its golden eyes as if to disparage her concern, for surely no mouse would be so foolish as to trespass this kitchen?

"Would ye speak with me?"

Hanna's heart tripped at the sound of Alex's voice. She both dreaded and anticipated his departure on King Alexander's orders in the morning. She wanted to spend the remaining hours locked in his arms—or, perhaps as far away as she could possibly manage. It seemed the air was too thick for her to breathe when she was in his presence. Would she find the courage to leave whilst he was away?

Setting her warring thoughts aside, she followed him into his solar. He closed the door and Hanna remembered her earlier wariness at being alone with him in this room. This time, she did not fear harm to her person, but the cost to her heart, for she was well aware it would take very little to tempt her back into his arms.

Maintaining her distance, she stared at the man before her. His tall form still showed the benefits of his active life. His upright stance, his head tilted at an angle that revealed the confidence of a man born to lead. Silver threads at his temples gave concession to the passage of youth, and though Hanna did not truly know his age, she suspected he was perhaps ten years her senior.

The cuff of his leine slipped back, revealing a scar that ran from the back of one hand up his forearm. Potentially a grievous wound, and if so, he'd overcome it completely, for she saw no weakness in him. Strength radiated from him. Stubbornness. Yes, she saw that in him, too. Much like Torvald, though the lines at the corners of Alex's mouth pulled his lips into smiles that melted her heart, while Torvald's lips had pushed often enough into frowns of frustration and impatience.

Alex closed the distance between them and claimed both her hands. He ran his thumbs across the backs of her hands and Hanna stared at them as the shock of his touch seared paths up each arm and pooled hot and low in her belly.

"I have come to realize why I dinnae trip over myself to take one of the young, lithesome lasses to wife soon after Annag died."

"Because ye were waiting for an older woman with no prospects, born on the wrong side of the border, and whose appearance is merely adequate?"

"Hanna!" Alex protested.

"I am considerably older than the maidens I saw in your hall a little over a month ago," Hanna pointed out. "I have but two gowns—only one of which is truly mine—no husband or family for protection," she added. "And ye cannot dispute my heritage."

Alex drew first one hand to his lips, then the other, dropping a gentle kiss to the back of each one. "Ye are so incredibly beautiful," he said. "So strong. My Valkyrie."

"Valkyrie?" Hanna repeated, startled at the image. "I do not hold sway over men's lives."

"Och, but ye do, sweet Hanna. Ye dinnae hesitate to author the end of that scoundrel's life on the dock that day, and ye certainly hold sway over my life. And my happiness."

"Alex, we've discussed this."

"Aye, we have," he agreed. "But I dinnae believe I said the right words."

"What makes ye think so?" she asked.

"Because ye havenae consented to becoming my wife."

Hanna shoved the pang of longing deep inside. "I have told ye my reasons. And unless Norway and Scotland have declared a truce, I will not argue the points. I will not make a suitable wife for ye, and I will not give ye my heart only to have ye return it when ye marry a Scottish woman as your council wishes."

"Hanna, I am leaving on the king's business in the morning. I would ask two things of ye."

Startled at his change in direction, Hanna nodded. "How may I help?"

"Peigi remains confined by the damp weather. Though the air is warm, the rains make her ache in a manner that keeps her abed. Gillian needs someone to look after her, and I would ask ye to do this."

"Certainly," Hanna replied. "I will care for her whilst ye are away."

"In truth, ye already have much of Gillian's care, and I am truly grateful."

Pleasure at his words heated Hanna's cheeks. "What is your second request?"

He paused, releasing one hand to settle the backs of his fingers against her cheek. Instinctively, Hanna leaned into the caress—and felt her world spin out of control.

* * *

Alex drew her close, wondering if she would resist him. To his surprise, her hesitation was brief, and he wrapped his arms about her.

"Promise ye will be here when I return," he said. "I will have nothing to worry me if I know ye wait for me here."

"I will not leave—ye know this. I have promised to care for Gillian."

"I want ye to wait for *me*," he growled, frustration fraying his temper. "Dinnae let some braw young man claim yer heart whilst I am gone."

"Och, Alex," Hanna whispered, "I cannot give away what does not belong to me."

"I cannae think straight when I hold ye like this," he grumbled. "Speak plainly."

"My heart belongs to ye. I have wished for it to be otherwise, but, it has not listened to reason."

"Then spend the night with me, Hanna. And I will have the marriage contract drawn up. We can marry upon my return."

"There are too many obstacles . . .."

He placed two fingers over her lips. "There are no obstacles save those ye echo endlessly back to me. I dinnae care if yer heritage is Norse. I have good relationships with many Norse. I dinnae care if ye give me a child or not. I may pick my heir as I please. Ye and I are of an age, though I daresay my summers far exceed yours."

He drew her with him until he reached the hearth, then sank to his knees before her.

"Ye are a beautiful, rare woman, Hanna. Give me this night to pleasure ye, and I will give ye every beat of my heart for the rest of my life."

Chapter Twenty

July 5, 1249

Alex ordered the ship away from the isle of Kerrera, gliding into Admucknish Bay as dusk fell. He stood patiently beside his king as Alexander pondered the imposing edifice of Dunstaffnage Castle. Its irregular shape matched no architect's plan, for the walls sat atop a mass of bedrock that cared naught for man's love of straight lines and even angles.

"MacDougall built this?" Alexander, King of Scotland, inquired pensively, rubbing a thumb and forefinger over his chin.

"Nearly a decade ago, Sire," Alex replied, hiding his concern for the spots of feverish color on the king's cheeks. It was rumored the king had fallen ill on the voyage, but he allowed none to question either his health or his plans. "Though the finishing of it has been recent."

"'Tis a brute piece of masonry," the king grunted. "Nary a window in sight, and the damn thing appears to have risen from the rock itself. How tall does yer information say the walls are?"

"Close to sixty feet, if ye count the rock beneath it."

"And likely ten feet thick." The king swore beneath his breath.

"Aye."

Silence drew a heavy veil over the conversation. At last King Alexander nodded.

"We will take the castle." With a wave of his hand, the king indicated their return to the Isle of Kerrera.

Alex bit back his questions. They were for the king's commanders and advisors, not him. If commanded to throw himself at the solid walls of Dunstaffnage, he would find a way to make things work in his men's favor. He would not disobey his king, but he would not sacrifice his soldiers for a doomed cause.

The next morning broke pale yellow and pearl pink through misted clouds. Alex hurried through the crowded campsite. King Alexander may have had a formidable fleet floating in Oban Bay, but he'd ordered a tent to be erected on the Isle of Kerrera, citing a desire for more space and a bed minus the toss of the waves. The ships' captains had been advised to ready the fleet, but no further instruction had arrived since the previous night, and Alex grew weary of the paucity of information, eager to return home.

A young man, likely in his early twenties—very early twenties if Alex was any judge—fell into step next to him as Alex approached the king's pavilion. His hair swung free, lightly brushing his shoulders, his demeanor confident, perhaps even cocky. But the most striking thing about him was his overly-embellished sword belt. Gems the size of coins winked from the sturdy leather, causing Alex to blink in surprise.

"Have ye been summoned as well?" the young man asked.

"Summoned? Nae. I merely wish to hear the day's orders," Alex replied, breaking free of the allure of the king's ransom in jewels. "Have ye the king's ear, then?"

"Och, I attend the king in a minor capacity whilst he is in Ayrshire, which he was—earlier, I mean." The man grinned, making him look even younger than his apparent age. "Piers de Curry," he added, extending a hand. "Sir Piers."

Alex gripped the young man's forearm briefly. Though he appeared a courtier, following at the king's heels, there was nothing soft about the muscle beneath the fabric of his leine. Sir Piers had obviously earned his title honestly.

"Alex MacLean, Chief of Clan MacLean."

120

Piers's eyes widened. "Sea trade? I have heard of ye."

Alex hid his pause. "Aye. I hope the king speaks kindly of me."

"Actually, His Majesty speaks *verra* highly of ye," Piers replied solemnly. "I would be honored if ye had time to give me a tour of yer ship."

Alex halted at the entrance to the king's tent with a nod to the guards who acknowledged them without challenge. "'Twould be my honor, but we should mayhap discuss this after we hear the king's plans." With a pleasant smile, he motioned for Piers to enter first. Polite, perhaps, but he had become aware of a noise not unlike an angry beehive just beyond the flaps, and Piers was, after all, the king's man.

Guards on the inside of the doorway stood at attention, half-straining to hear what the king and his counselors argued so vehemently over, half-straining to be the first out the door should calamity strike. Alex couldn't say he blamed them. The king in a royal fit was a daunting sight.

King Alexander strode back and forth, eyebrows furrowed together and lips pursed tight in an unhappy expression, his heavy velvet robe flapping behind him in the breeze of his stomping passage. Two commanders Alex recognized from introductions a day earlier leaned over the king's desk, shoulders squared, fists braced on the smooth worktop, resoluteness etched in their posture. A third reclined in a padded chair, a forefinger tapping his chin in a thoughtful gesture.

At Alex's and Piers's entrance, the king whirled, jabbing a finger at Alex.

"What do ye have to say about this?" he shouted.

Taken aback, Alex bowed deeply before replying calmly. "If Your Majesty could enlighten me?"

The king huffed and threw himself into the massive chair

behind the desk, his face flushed, moisture beading on his forehead. He motioned Alex to approach. Piers followed on his heels. Both bowed deeply, though the king took little notice, such was his agitation.

"I am prepared to send forces against MacDougall," King Alexander began with a scowl at the other three men who carefully averted their gazes. "And yet, last night, I had a dream."

Something stirred in Alex's chest, a flicker of unease, or perhaps a chill of premonition. He said nothing, and impressed, noted young Piers kept silent as well.

"I was visited by three men," the king began. His voice trailed off thoughtfully. After a moment, he shook his head. "One was dressed in royal robes." His gaze drifted to Piers who appeared the most elegantly-clad man in the receiving tent. "But verra stern, with a ruddy complexion. The second, a slender man, was verra engaging and majestic. The last was of verra great stature and his features were distorted."

A small groan came from some man in the room and the king glanced up sharply. No one moved or offered apology. Clearing his throat, the king continued.

"Each inquired if I intended to invade the Isles." Blustering, as if seeking approval for or defense of his intended actions, King Alexander rose from his chair and resumed pacing. "Of course, I replied I had every intention of doing so. 'Tis past time to subject the Isles to Scotland's rule."

The king strode about in silence, his head thrust forward belligerently, a frown etched on his face. After several moments, Alex ventured his question.

"What was their response, Sire?"

King Alexander whipped about, his face leached white. "They bade me turn back. Insisted no other measure would turn to my advantage." Sudden color flooded his cheeks. "Blasted dream!" He waved an arm at his commanders. "Blasted advisors! Ye fall apart at the least set-back."

"Sire, this is scarcely a set-back," one of the commanders blustered.

"Bah! Ye arenae soldier material! Frightened lasses, the lot of ye. I asked for advice, and I get naught but a stampede for the nearest door." He again addressed Alex. "What say ye?"

Alex contemplated his sovereign for a moment, then studied the carpet at his feet. A costly tapestry, easily the work of years, bunched beneath his boots. Stories of visions unheeded flashed through his memory. Cautionary tales of thwarting a king shoved to the forefront of his mind.

"Sire," he began. "If I may be so bold as to point out, ye sailed with me yester eve, and we both viewed Dunstaffnage. The site is well-chosen, the walls thick and high. Though I have nae doubt ye can take the castle, I believe the cost will be high."

King Alexander stared at Alex a long, nerve-wracking moment. Silence crackled in the room, tension heating Alex's blood.

Suddenly, the king snapped his fingers. "Piers, attend me."

Striding angrily between his advisors and guards, the king stalked from the tent. Tossing a wide-eyed look and faint shoulder shrug to Alex, Piers followed at the king's heels.

The tent's flaps billowed in the king's wake. Tension thickened within the room as the remaining men eyed each other cautiously. One of the commanders broke free of his stance at the king's desk.

"I am nae weak-willed doom-sayer," he informed the small group. "But if I were attended by saints Olave, Magnus and Columba—"

"The king said naught of their names," Alex interrupted.

"Did ye nae listen to him?" the second commander asked.

"Royally robed, stern and red of face—it couldnae be other than St. Olave!"

"And St. Magnus was a slender man, verra majestic," the first added.

"Do ye call the third man St. Columba because of his great size, then?" the man in the chair drawled. He rose, brushing the hem of his leine straight before gathering his cloak. "I cannae say I concur with the appropriation of these particular saints in the king's dream, but I dinnae doubt he has had severe reservations—which haunted him yester eve." He lowered his voice. "Reservations and a high fever."

Personally, Alex considered lingering doubts after viewing the massive MacDougall stronghold the most likely cause of the king's dream, though it was never prudent to discount Divine Providence when such a battle loomed before them. But the first two commanders had resumed muttering between themselves and clearly had no desire to take up arms before such a show in the form of not one, but *three* venerated saints. Their opinions could hardly be swayed.

"Care for a bit of fresh air?" the third commander asked, wry humor in the tilt of one brow. "Clearly ye are as yet undecided what to make of the king's dream, and I would hear yer thoughts."

Alex cast another glance at the others, deep in fevered discussion, and nodded. They exited the tent into midmorning sun, the camp abuzz, no doubt from the king's stormy departure only a few moments earlier. Alex glanced quickly about and finally spied the king, Piers a half-stride behind his shoulder, two more men— likely aides-de-camp—stomping across the grass just beyond the perimeter of the camp. Four soldiers flanked them at a discrete distance.

"What do ye know of Dunstaffnage Castle?" Alex's companion

asked.

"'Tis a monstrosity of coarse rubble with sandstone dressing built directly onto the bedrock," Alex replied.

"No possibility of tunneling beneath?"

Alex shook his head.

"Scaling the walls?"

"Nearly sixty feet in height most places," Alex replied in a thoughtful manner.

His companion opened his mouth, but a cry spread through the camp like a lit match to oil, interrupting their desultory conversation.

"The king! The king!"

Alex surged forward, shoving men aside without heed to rank or privilege. Within moments, he arrived on the edge of camp. The king's guards hurried, four-square, carrying a prone figure in their midst. Piers led the group of aides swarming in the king's wake.

A path opened before the guards as they bore the king to his tent. Necks strained to catch a glimpse of the proceedings. Voices raised in speculation and misinformation.

Alex formed into the procession next to Piers. The man's face bore not a trace of color, and though he stared fixedly at the ground, he stumbled over each rock and clod.

"Steady," Alex murmured, clapping a hand to Piers's shoulder.

Piers shot him a grateful look, and Alex noted again the youth of the man evident in the wide-eyed uncertainty.

He reminds me of myself. Alex's grim thought brought no humor with it. Life had once been carefree, dancing easily to his cocky tune. All too soon reality had raised its harsh head, and it appeared Piers was feeling the bitter sting.

The guards bore the king inside his tent and the flaps closed behind them, blocking further passage. Alex grabbed Piers's arm and dragged him aside.

"What happened?"

The young man gulped several times and scuffed a boot in the dirt. His chest heaved like a set of bellows as he sucked in air, and after a few moments, he settled enough to speak.

"He simply collapsed."

"Collapsed? There wasnae arrow, stone, other projectile?"

Piers shook his head. Alex stared at him narrowly. "Ye are certain?"

"They will find nothing," Piers declared, raising his upturned palms waist-high in supplication. "His Majesty stomped about for a bit, blustering about dreams making twittering lasses of perfectly braw men. I stood to one side, out of his way—as did the others—and, he fell."

"Fell?"

"Collapsed, dropped," Piers sighed, exhaling the shock on a long breath. "He dinnae trip over a grass clod or turn his ankle on a loose stone. He simply fell to the ground and dinnae move again."

Alex rubbed the back of his neck. The king's healer would soon determine if an assassination had been attempted—or, God forbid, accomplished.

"Come. Let us grab a bite to eat. 'Tis likely to be a long day."

Alex led an unresisting Piers to a nearby campfire and appropriated a trencher of warmed-over oatcakes and cider. They settled against a pair of large stones and ate, though Alex hardly tasted the food or drink.

"Ye believe 'twill be long before we know—something?" Piers ventured through a mouthful of bannocks.

Alex nodded. "If the king has taken to his bed, we will hear something soon enough. After that, who knows? We will likely not be disbanded until the king agrees, though after a bit, 'twill become difficult to continue feeding this many soldiers. "Tis my hope he will either recover quickly or be removed to Ayr for further treatment. Either course will settle our options—one way or another."

Around them, men shouted and grumbled, proclaiming brusquely of their intent to roust the MacDougalls from Dunstaffnage Castle and avenge their king. Tempers ran high, and fights broke out from time-to-time, which Alex and Piers observed but carefully avoided.

As the sun dipped lower, Alex stood atop a hillock, observing the sun's descent. A cry behind him startled his gloomy thoughts of time spent waiting to hear word of their next move. As the words caught his ears, he stiffened, then returned at a run to the camp.

"The king is dead!"

Chapter Twenty One

Hanna nodded her thanks to the messenger who returned a small bow before leaving her alone to read Alex's missive.

*I cannot go into detail here, but it
will be common knowledge soon
enough that the king is dead.*

Dead? Numb with shock, Hanna sank onto the bench behind her, the noise of the hall fading away.

How? Had there been a battle? Alex!

She quickly scanned the remainder of the note.

*I am well, though compelled to
return to Scone for the crowning of his
son as king. Poor lad is but eight
summers, and certain to be bewildered
by the loss of his father. I dinnae envy
him the life ahead of false flattery and
intrigue.*

*This means I will be at least a
month returning to ye. We will dock in
the Bishopric of Glasgow and move
overland to Scone, returning by the
same route. It is a long journey, but
one that must be made.*

Do ye think of me, Hanna? Do ye

remember our night together—the feel
of your skin on mine? The shuddering
collapse as ye reach as far as ye can
and splinter into a thousand fragments
of passion? Though these past few
days have been difficult, I endure
sleepless nights with yer memory. I
cannot wait to be in your arms, see
your sweet face.
Give Gillian a hug and kiss from
me. Let Edan know he is still in charge
in my absence, and why.
Alex

Hanna's fingertips brushed the missive, then drifted to her lips as though the parchment conveyed Alex's touch to her.

So, the king of Scotland is dead. She scanned the parchment again, but Alex had included no details. No information on whether King Alexander had died in battle or of another cause. She drifted slowly to the stairwell, eyes drinking in the details he *had* provided. How could that night affect her so? And Alex as well, if his words were any indication. Lazy tendrils of passion flowed through her at the memories his missive invoked.

She halted at the edge of the room as someone called her name. Placing the parchment against her breast, she waited for Edan's approach.

"Have ye heard from Alex?" he asked. Nearly a sennight had passed without word, and he shared Hanna's worry. Though certain bad news would have traveled quickly, there could be many reasons there had been no report—few of them good.

"Aye." Hanna motioned him to an empty corner of the room.

"The king is dead."

Edan's eyes widened, and he sucked in a hissing breath. "Shite!" He gestured for the parchment, but Hanna shook her head.

"'Tis all he says about it, except he is on his way to Scone to see to the coronation of the new king." Her cheeks heated. "The rest is mine alone."

Edan's eyebrows jerked up in surprise. "As ye will."

"He says to tell ye 'twill likely be a month before his return, and for ye to continue in his absence."

"The trip to Scone from here isnae easy," Edan mused, rubbing his chin. "I wonder if they'll sail to Glasgow and go overland from there."

"Aye. He said he would leave the *Porpoise* in Glasgow."

"Och, then we will simply settle in and await his return." Edan's smile eased Hanna's fears a small degree. "Dinnae fash. He will be all the more anxious to be home after his lengthy absence."

Hanna watched Edan's retreating back, musing over her reaction to Alex's final words. He clearly had every intention of furthering their relationship once he returned to Morvern. Despite— or perhaps because of—her strong feelings for the MacLean Laird, she could not allow that to happen.

* * *

Alex shifted his weight to ease the abuse to his buttocks from the bony back of the horse he'd procured in Glasgow as it bumped its way over the muddy road to Scone. Following the king's procession left them to manage the mired trails as best they could. His plaide draped over his head, keeping out most of the rain, but the constant drizzle sent rivulets of water dripping off the edge of the heavy fabric to pool in his lap. He pulled the wool closer and thought of Hanna and the night before he'd boarded the *Porpoise*.

What is yer favorite memory of yer daughter? He didn't know why he wanted to know about Hanna's daughter. Perhaps it was because he had one himself, and Hanna's stories, hesitant at first, seemed to bring them closer together.

She was but four summers and fascinated with the plants growing in the garden. She wanted so much to help, and I showed her the difference between the herbs and weeds. I found her early one morn with my sewing scissors, snipping all the tops off the weeds. She said it was faster and not as messy as pulling them up by their roots.

Hanna's eyes had softened and she'd sighed as she leaned her head against his shoulder.

Signy. Her name meant New Victory, and it suited her. She seemed to accomplish something new every day. Such a busy child. So much like your Gillian.

His nag stumbled, jerking Alex from his thoughts. Words rumbled back through the ranks, heralding their arrival.

Scone!

The King is dead!

Long live the King!

* * *

Alex slept deeply, rousing only when the rumbling of his stomach was out-distanced by the need to relieve his bladder. He crept from his narrow bed in the abbey's tiny room. After he made use of the chamber pot, he dressed and stalked the corridors until he found Piers and his men sitting at the entrance to the abbey.

"Food," he commanded. "I don't care where we find it, but 'tis first on our schedule this morn."

One of his men pulled a packet of dried beef and bannocks from his sporran. "'Twill be all ye get this morn," he said. "The town is overrun with people and short on supplies. None expected this."

Alex ruefully accepted the morsel of meat and a handful of oatcakes. Someone else passed him a water flask and he settled down to eat.

"The young king will be crowned on the morrow," Piers mentioned. "There is to be a banquet tonight for the gathered lords to mark the passing of the king. The celebration on the morrow will be more festive—in honor of the new."

"Poor lad," added a soldier. "He's not old enough to take on the ambitions of Walter Comyn."

"The earl should keep watch on Alan Durward," another replied. "He, too, desires the young king's ear."

"The lad will feel the struggle," Alex said. "I dinnae envy him the throne." He peered at the sky, slate gray to mourn the passing of the king. "Mayhap we should be about the town for a bit before finding our seats in the palace. I, for one, will be glad to honor the king's memory with a hearty meal."

They paid little heed to the drizzle that beaded fuzzily on their plaides. Alex found a goodwife making the best of the crowd by selling berry pasties, and managed to buy enough to satisfy himself, Piers, and the four men in his personal guard. By the time they entered the hall for the banquet, the excitement of the crowd had risen to a fever pitch, and they were glad to find their seats at the long tables.

Servants scurried about, filling flasks, mugs and cups, and loading the tables with venison, whole roast pigs, roasted vegetables and freshly baked bread. Alex was soon full and drowsy, overly warm in the crowded hall. He leaned against the wall at his back, surveying the people. Lasses wiped up the spills as men over-indulged and misjudged the angle of the table. Lads struggled beneath platters of discarded bones—those which didn't make it to the hounds littering the floor—feathers and skin from the redressed peacock, and mussel shells sucked dry of their succulent contents.

Alex nudged Piers. "Have ye sailed much?" he asked as they lingered in the hall.

"A bit," Piers replied. "My family lives in Ayrshire, and I have been known to board a ship or two." He sent Alex an eager grin. "An opportunity to sail to the Mediterranean is verra exciting!"

"I am glad to assist," Alex replied. He had alleviated some of the tension of the journey by regaling Piers with tales of pirates and far-off lands and finished by offering him a berth when *Alacrity* made her maiden voyage to Spain in a few weeks.

His head turned as a serving lass passed the table, her hair bound in a kerchief, golden strands escaping to frame her face.

"Do ye find blonde women attractive?" Piers asked absently, his eyes tracking the woman. "She appears Norse, and likely an easy conquest." He shrugged. "I have encountered such refugees before and they have been eager for coin and a bit of fun."

"She is but a lass," Alex growled. "She should be treated with respect."

"I dinnae mean to *force* her," Piers protested. "Does it make a difference so long as she's willing?"

Alex remembered Hanna's generosity and trust. "All the difference in the world."

Piers grunted. "She is likely a slave, from the looks of her. Poor lass dinnae escape the raiders. I've heard most wind up on the auction block in Rome and beyond." Piers rose from the bench and stretched, then straightened his tunic. His jeweled belt glistened in the torchlight. "I will see ye at the coronation," he said. "Dinnae wait up for me."

Alex dismissed Piers from his mind. There was no changing the young man. Likely, the lasses vied for his attentions, and it clearly did not occur to him not all women welcomed his advances. He thumped the table, marking his decision to leave. He would not watch drunken men prey on the serving women, willing or not.

"I dinnae wish to linger," he said, his men nodding in agreement. The serving lass turned, the sound of his knuckles on the worn boards clear even in the noisy room.

"My lord?" she questioned. Alex stared at her, mouth open in shock.

"It cannae be!"

Her eyes, a vibrant green Alex recognized, widened. Her golden hair glided across her soft cheeks, her skin pale.

Alex rose, stalked to the end of the table, his eyes pinning the lass in place. She stiffened and her fingers fluttered across her sleeve before she glanced down with a scowl.

She is used to a dagger in her sleeve. Alex's heart raced. *She looks exactly like Hanna.*

"*Hva heter du?*" he demanded, certain how she would answer.

The girl's green eyes widened, glistening as fear and hope mingled to bring tears to the surface.

"*Jeg heter* Signy," she whispered. "Torvaldsdottir. Do I know ye?"

Chapter Twenty Two

Alex leaned over the rails, breathing the rich aroma of the forests closing on either side of the ship as they entered the Strait of Mull. It was good to be home, and his thoughts wandered from the coronation of the new king a few days earlier. Alexander III had held up well to the ceremonies and flattery attending his crowning and seemed appreciative to receive the MacLean's allegiance.

Poor bairn. He'll either grow vexed with the false flattery of his courtiers soon and begin making his own decisions—to their dismay—or lose himself in the mysteries and back-stabbing that are castle politics.

Alex's gaze drifted to the lass who had occupied the extra cabin during their trip, and who now stood at the rail several feet away, facing the wind, excitement radiating from every line of her body. Alex grinned. He was as impatient to return home as was Signy. He'd never bought a slave before, though he'd encountered enough of them when he lived in the Holy Land, and he'd immediately given the lass her freedom.

Understandably wary of him in the beginning, she soon warmed to him—and Piers, whom he'd had to warn off with a parental shake of his head. Anticipating her joy at seeing her ma again filled him with a fierce pleasure, and he couldn't wait to see the look on Hanna's face when they arrived at Morvern.

"Ye truly plan to marry this lass's ma? A Norsewoman?" Piers shrugged. "She must have bewitched ye to risk angering the king."

"My allegiance to the king doesnae extend to my bedroom," Alex drawled. "Ye will meet Hanna soon enough." Alex paused.

"She hasnae said she will marry me."

Sails snapped in the wind and Alex was glad of the fair weather. Hanna and Signy deserved to reunite beneath a sun-kissed sky, not a sodden downpour. He peered at the horizon, spying the smudge of land beckoning them to Morvern's docks. Excitement rose. Sailors leapt about as they prepared to bring the ship to harbor. Soldiers, weary of the long journey, shouted encouragement.

Signy turned to Alex. "Is this home?"

* * *

"The laird's ship approaches!"

Excited voices lifted and Hanna wiped her hands on her apron. Dread quickly dampened her happiness at the news, for she would allow herself naught more than relief Laird MacLean had returned safely. The past weeks had taught her that giving him up at some future date to the woman who would bear his name—and hopefully his heir—was not something she could endure.

I am but a passing novelty to him, but I could only love with my whole heart.

Using a bit of woolen cloth discarded from the weaver's loom, Hanna had packed away her few belongings when word reached them the laird was headed home. Hanging from the peg behind the door of the room she and Aadny shared, the precious russet cloak hanging next to it, the bag was ready to make the trip to wherever she could start anew. Dunstaffnage was the logical choice, as she was certain she would find other Norse refugees there as well.

A mocking voice intruded on her thoughts.

Alex welcomed ye when he did not have to, and when a less just man would have imprisoned ye—or worse.

Hanna frowned. *I leave to protect myself, not to rebuke him.*

Gillian's shrieks reached Hanna long before the child herself. Moments later Gillian swung through the door, loping across the room in great bounds.

"Da is home! Did ye hear, Hanna? Da is home!"

"I believe I heard some such rumor," Hanna said. "Did ye wish to greet him at the dock?"

Gillian bobbed up and down in elation. "Aye!"

"Mayhap Aadny should go with ye. Her feet can keep up with ye better." Hanna turned to the young girl who had arrived on Gillian's heels. "Take the child to her da before she bursts at the seams."

Aadny grabbed Gillian's hand. "Let's go," she cried, as caught up in the excitement as the rest of the clan, and they bounded out the door. Hanna's eyes clouded with tears.

"*Ha det bra, skatten min,*" she whispered. *Good-bye, my treasure. Ye will always be in my heart. Ye will forget me in time, and another will take my place.*

Hanna hurried to retrieve her bag, certain her heart lay in a thousand pieces in Gillian's wake. She stumbled on the stair and wiped her eyes with her sleeve. Careful to navigate the hall in its shadowed margins, she slipped through the door without attracting attention. People thronged the bailey and the road through the village, the air festive. The clan had mourned the loss of the king, but their laird had at last returned and they eagerly awaited news from Scone.

The crowd slowed Hanna's pace, and worry pricked at her.

How long before I am missed? It was certain Gillian would waste no time seeking her. But would her father? Hanna had heard nothing from him after the single missive. Understandable, but she had no inclination to pursue their relationship and could not risk waiting to discover his intent. Weeks had passed. Hearts were oft times fickle. It was possible he'd met someone—a woman of noble Scottish birth—who would make a better match than a penniless

Norsewoman.

Hanna's heart twisted and she knew she made the best decision. If she remained, she doomed herself to heartbreak far beyond the tears she would shed at leaving Gillian behind.

The noise of the crowd increased.

Blast! How did they disembark so quickly? Hanna glanced about, seeking a place to hide to let the laird's party pass. She backed into an empty doorway, making the most of the shadows. People packed against her, straining to see. After a moment, Alex rode into view.

Edan must have placed horses at the pier. Of course, he'd make this more a triumphal entry rather than a simple walk from the ship. Hanna rolled her eyes.

Gillian sat on a horse next to him, Aadny close behind her. A young man Hanna did not know rode next to Alex, sunlight sparking from a magnificent jeweled belt. On a third horse sat a young woman—a girl, really—and Hanna's worst fears were realized. She averted her gaze, unwilling to look upon the child-bride Alex MacLean had brought home to marry.

* * *

Alex scanned the crowd, hoping not to trample anyone in his haste to make it to the castle, to prove to Signy her ma was here—to give Hanna something she did not expect. He almost shushed Gillian's excited chatter, but knew she was only glad to see him. He lifted his gaze—and saw Hanna.

Though her face was turned away and half-hidden in shadow, he had no doubt who she was. But, why had she not accompanied Gillian? Why did she skulk in the doorway? His gaze noted the bag clutched in one hand.

She is leaving? No! Reining his horse to an abrupt halt, he tossed the reins to Piers and leapt to the ground. A path through the throng opened magically before him. He halted before Hanna, his heart pained at the thought of her betrayal.

"Ye promised to wait," he said, pitching his voice low. Hanna's green eyes pierced his soul.

"Ye promised ye would not marry," she replied, her voice weary.

He stared at her. "What are ye talking about? I havenae married."

"No? Then ye should marry her before her kin accuse ye of seducing an innocent." Her eyes blazed. "I told ye I wouldnae stand by and watch ye marry. Just because she is too young to bed does not mean I will serve in her place!"

Alex drew back, at a loss as to what had stirred Hanna up. What rumor named him such a blackguard? And what woman—lass—did she refer to?

He was suddenly aware of the silence of the crowd.

"*Mútta?*"

Chapter Twenty Three

Hanna's head jerked, her gaze searching the crowd. "What devilment have ye wrought?" she hissed. "What have ye done?"

"No devilment, Hanna, other than by the men who raided yer village." Alex trapped her shoulder in one hand, stilling her movements. "I brought ye a wee gift from Scone."

Signy slammed into Hanna, knocking the breath completely from her. Her daughter's slender arms gripped her waist, her beloved face buried in Hanna's cloak. Shrieking sobs tore from the girl's throat. Hanna's head wobbled in disbelief and she sucked in huge gasps of air.

"Oh! Oh!" she cried. "Oh!" Hanna crumpled to the ground, pulling her daughter onto her lap, holding her tight. She rocked back and forth, crooning as tears rolled down her cheeks.

Alex noted Edan and his guard formed a protective arc around them, pressing the curious throng back, using the horses to help create a barrier to block their view. Gillian and Aadny stepped within.

He swallowed against the large lump in his throat and wiped the back of one hand across his eyes. He had removed three children from his grieving wife's arms and held back his tears. This reunion threatened to send him to his knees.

Hanna and Signy remained locked in a fervent embrace, and the crowd, determining their curiosity would have to be appeased later, began to disperse. Alex knelt beside Hanna. Gillian tucked a small hand in his.

"Is she happy, Da?" she whispered, concern wrinkling her face.

Alex pulled her close, patting her back reassuringly. "I believe she is, *leannan*. We will give them time to get used to being together again, aye?"

Gillian nodded, her worried gaze easing slightly. She slipped from Alex's side and hunkered next to Hanna. Laying a palm on Hanna's shoulder, she simply waited.

The slight weight of Gillian's hand recalled Hanna to the present. She lifted her head and gave Gillian a wobbly smile. Her throat was too swollen to speak, her head too fuzzy to hold a coherent thought. She swallowed and gave her attention to Alex.

"Where . . . ?" she whispered.

"I found her working as a . . . serving lass at Scone Palace."

Signy shifted against Hanna's shoulder. "Searc's men searched the long house before he torched it. He said we would bring him much money."

Hanna's heart hardened, not liking the easy way her daughter spoke of the man who'd kidnapped her. "Searc? Do ye know of him, Alex MacLean?"

He nodded. "I do, but before ye plot yer revenge, I will tell ye he met his end in a brawl not long after he and his men raided yer village. I left two men in Scone to see what they could uncover. Searc led a group of clanless men who pirated up and down the coast. If any yet live, my men will track them down."

Hanna's blood cried out for vengeance—*her* vengeance. And yet, it was satisfying to know Alex had done what he could to bring the men to justice.

"Will ye come home, Hanna?" Alex asked. "Ye and Signy are free to go where ye will," he glanced at his daughter. "But Gillian and I want ye to come home."

Home? Just when Hanna thought she had no tears left to shed, more prickled her eyes, springing from a different spot deep inside.

Tears for Signy had wrenched hot and bitter from the grief she'd not emptied, the shock and relief at seeing her.

These tears tasted of hope.

"Is it true ye are going to marry him?" Signy whispered, dipping her chin to indicate Alex.

Hanna's lips twitched. "He has asked."

"What did ye say?"

Hanna stared at Alex's expectant face. "I said there were too many obstacles. That his people would not accept me. That I was not the right woman for him."

Signy's gaze slid to Alex. "Then, why did he save me?"

Alex offered his hand and Hanna placed her fingers within his strong, sure grasp. He lifted her to her feet, his gaze compelling Hanna to listen to his answer.

"Because, Hanna, I would do anything to bring ye joy."

The final strand of reluctance, of anger and distrust, broke away. For a moment, Hanna was adrift, the purpose she'd clung to gone. Signy squeezed her hand. Gillian leaned against her legs. Alex smiled. Mischief entered Hanna's heart.

"I don't know," she murmured, tilting her head to Signy. "He's rather old. And often gone from home."

Signy giggled. Gillian startled, then entered the game.

"He's always stealing pasties," she sighed. "But he has nice knees!"

Hanna and Aadny burst out laughing. Signy and Alex exchanged glances with a shrug. Gillian looked smug. Alex pulled Hanna close.

"Ride with me?" he asked.

Knowing where he would take her, and no longer fearful for her heart, Hanna nodded.

* * *

"Piers is certain ye have bewitched me," Alex murmured against her hair. He twined a lock of her hair about his forefinger.

"We Norse have been Christians for quite a few years now," Hanna replied sleepily. "But not so long we have forgotten the old ways."

"Ye will marry me, aye? I'd hate to be thrown over for a younger man in a few years." The hay whispered as he shifted on their makeshift bed. "And why do my knees make ye laugh?"

Hanna chuckled. "'Tis from a bedtime tale. The woman chose her husband based solely on his knees. She chose unwisely."

"Marrying me is the wise thing to do, Hanna. I swear it."

Hanna rose over him, her golden hair falling in a curtain about them. Alex plucked a strand of fragrant hay from a burnished lock.

"Do ye swear to love me when I do not grow round with child? Though I have not ceased my courses, I have but two children—the last nine summers ago. Will ye love me when others whisper behind your back that ye married beneath ye—that ye married a Norsewoman?"

Alex swept one of her arms aside and rolled, reversing their positions. "I will love ye even when ye grow fat with my child. And I will laugh to know I made the right decision to marry my Valkeryie." He moved over her, settling between her thighs. Hanna wrapped her legs about his waist.

"I will not bring shame to ye," she said. "And I will not step aside for another."

"I trust ye," Alex said as he nudged against her. Hanna gasped and adjusted to accept him. "And none will come between us. This I swear."

Epilogue

May, 1250
MacLean Castle

A heavy mist hung in the air, clinging to the final chill of winter. It had been such a morning when she'd awakened to the last day of her life in Hällstein. The rousing bark of the dogs was but a fading memory, and though she closed her eyes in regret that after long months of searching, no trace of her son, Sten, had been found, there was much to rejoice over.

Alex gently stroked her arm.

"'Twas a year ago, was it not?"

Hanna pushed away the memory with little more than a faint pang of regret. It no longer held the raw agony of a fresh wound, but rather the thoughtful line of a fading scar. Noted, but often ignored.

"Aye. A year ago raiders destroyed my life." She turned her face into his hand, placing a kiss on his palm. "And I have a new life now, for which I am exceedingly grateful." She rose from the bed and, pulling a robe from the foot of the bed, moved quietly to the cradle next to the hearth.

"Who could imagine such a blessing?"

Alex joined her, wrapping his arms about her waist. He rested his chin on her shoulder and stared at the small form sleeping peacefully.

"He is more than I dared hope for," Alex replied. "All I truly wanted was ye. This lad is a great boon."

"Ye dinnae mind having a bairn in your old age?" Hanna teased.

Alex growled softly and nudged his fully erect cock against her buttocks. "I am of a mind to see if we could create another, dear wife," he said. "Do ye think wee Birk will sleep a bit longer? I'd like to linger over his ma."

Hanna swiveled within the circle of his arms. "I'm all for lingering," she whispered.

"Truth? It hasnae been long since his birth."

Hanna nibbled at his lower lip. "Aye, but it has been long enough."

~The End~

A NOTE FROM THE AUTHORS

We'd like to thank you for joining us for Alex MacLean's Happy-ever-after. His story bridges the gap between The Highlander's Crusader Bride, which opens in 1221 CE, and The Highlander's Welsh Bride, which takes place in 1282 CE after the fall of Prince Llywelyn at the Battle of Orewin Bridge. If you're interested in the historical parts of The Highlander's Norse Bride, read on...

King Alexander II's death occured pretty much as you read in our story (except for literary license at putting Alex—and possibly Piers—in the tale). Scottish accounts have the king dying of a mysterious fever, while Norse accounts state he died of Divine Retribution. Either way, he did (reportedly) have a dream that cautioned him against attacking Ewan MacDougall, whom King Haakon had appointed as King of the Isles, and he did die on the Isle of Kererra before he realized his dream of wresting control of the Isles and western Scotland from the hands of King Haakon of Norway.

As a historical side note: In 1158, Somerled joined a rebellion to overthrow Godfrey the Black, a heavy-handed and very unpopular ruler of the Isle of Man and the Hebrides. Though the title King of the Isles dated back hundreds of years prior to Godfrey, all had owed their allegiance to the King of Norway. Somerled claimed the title, but created a third force in the long-standing conflict between Scotland and Norway, declaring himself independant of both countries. However, in 1164, Somerled died in battle with Malcolm IV's army. Neither Malcolm nor the King of Norway approved Somerled's lack of allegiance, and eventually put an end to his claim. Somerled's kingdom was divided between his sons, and the struggle between Norway and Scotland continued. The title *Lord of the Isles* would be in common useage in the mid 1300's.

Piers de Curry was one of those characters who often gets discovered along the way—and one of those things we love about research. In 1263 at the Battle of Largs, when Scottish and Norse forces finally met in battle, Sir Piers de Curry was one of the few combatants who died that day. He was distinguished by his helmet and armor which was inlaid with gold and jewels, and conspicuous because of his courage. He tried repeatedly to provoke the Norsemen into battle by riding down to their ranks and taunting them.

We gave him a spot in our story because we felt such a colorful character should have a second chance at history. And, by sending him to Spain on one of Alex MacLean's ships, we gave him the journey by which he attained some of his fabulous armor and the Spanish charger he was said to ride.

Unfortunately, his bravery in battle was short-lived. After heckling the Norse, one of their commanders, Andrew Nikolson, became fed up with him and swung his sword with such might that he sliced through Piers' armor, not only cleaving through his thigh, but making a dent in his saddle as well. After that, it is said the worst of the battle was over Piers's gold and jewels which the Norse took as bounty. (Sorry, history doesn't always have an HEA.)

The Norse, who had arrived on Scotland's shores with an armada and the intent to put an end to Scotland's ambitions over the Isles, had lost much of its fleet in a terrible storm, and hoped in vain for the arrival of fresh troops. With ships stranded on the shore, broken upon the rocks or badly damaged after colliding with other vessels adrift in the waters off the coast of Ayrshire, and with the shore littered with corpses and drifted tackle, King Haakon asked for a truce to bury their dead—and also set fire to any ships that could not be used. King Haakon then retired to Orkney for the winter, intending to rejoin the battle in the spring, but died on Orkney that December.

Thus ended the Battle of Largs and Norway's dominion of the Western Isles. Three years later, King Haakon's son formally gave up the Hebrides and the Isle of Man to Scotland in exchange for an outright payment of 4000 marks and an annual payment according to the Treaty of Perth, though Norway retained rule over the Shetland and Orkney Islands.

The Norse jarls, as the Earls of Caithness, owed their allegiance to both Norway and the Scottish crown. In 1379, the earldom passed to the Sinclair family—Katja Sinclair's family in *The Highlander's Viking Bride*.

ACKNOWLEDGEMENTS

A huge thank you to my critique partners who read through this story in its varied permutations as Hanna and Alex's story evolved-Dawn Marie Hamilton, Cate Parke. And much gratitude to our wonderful beta group; Sharon, April, Mary, Donna, Cate, Ann, Cheryl, Barb, and RaeRae.

A million thanks go to our fab cover artist, Dar Albert!

If you enjoyed Alex and Hanna's story, please consider leaving a review. Thank you!

Other Books by Cathy & DD MacRae

The Hardy Heroine series

Highland Escape (book 1)
The Highlander's Viking Bride (book 2)
The Highlander's Crusader Bride (book 3)
The Highlander's Norse Bride, a Novella (book 4)
The Highlander's Welsh Bride (book 5)
The Prince's Highland Bride (book 6, available 2020)

by DD MacRae
The Italian Billionaire's Runaway Bride

By Cathy MacRae

The Highlander's Bride series

The Highlander's Accidental Bride (book 1)
The Highlander's Reluctant Bride (book 2)
The Highlander's Tempestuous Bride (book 3)
The Highlander's Outlaw Bride (book 4)
The Highlander's French Bride (book 5)

The Ghosts of Culloden Moor series
(with LL Muir, et al)

Adam
Malcolm
MacLeod
Patrick

De Wolfe Pack Connected Worlds
From Wolfebane Publishing

The Saint
The Penitent
The Cursed

About the Authors

Cathy MacRae lives on the sunny side of the Arbuckle Mountains where she and her husband read, write, and tend the garden—with the help of the dogs, of course.

You can visit with her on Facebook, or read her blogs and learn about her books at www.cathymacraeauthor.com. Drop her a line— she loves to hear from readers!

To keep up with new releases and other fun things, sign up for her newsletter! There's an easy form on her website. (You'll find DD's news there, too!)

DD MacRae enjoys bringing history to life. Research is one of the best things about writing a story! And with more than 35 years of martial arts training, DD also brings believable, breath-taking action to the tales.

You can connect with DD through www.cathymacraeauthor.com. It's always exciting to hear from readers!

READ A SHORT EXCERPT FROM THE HIGHLANDER'S WELSH BRIDE

(book 5 in the Hardy Heroines series)

Battle of Orewin Bridge, Wales
December 1282

Three English soldiers emerged from the woods, making enough noise to raise the dead. Carys caught her brother's arm in warning, but it was too late.

"Stop!" one of the soldiers shouted, drawing his sword. He burst across the small glen, the other two men at his heels.

Hywel snatched his bow from his shoulder. "Take the one on the left." In a swift move born of too much practice killing the English, he nocked and released an arrow, dropping the lead soldier in his tracks.

Carys flung her javelin, striking her target in the chest, piercing his leather armor and knocking him to the ground. The instant her hands were free, she drew her bow, aiming for the third Englishman whom Hywel had already staggered with an arrow. She added a feathered shaft of her own to ensure he fell and stayed down. Drawing her short sword, she stalked the bodies.

"Carys, we must fly!" Hywel called softly. "The prince has fallen. More of Longshank's men will be upon us anon."

The scream of steel on steel and of men dying rose on the air behind them, adding urgency to his plea. Carys nodded, pausing to stuff the few coins the dead English soldiers had in their possession, along with their daggers, into the small pack she carried. She spotted a silver necklace and yanked it over the head of its owner. A fine silver ring with beautiful filigree work set with an amber stone hung from the chain. She hastily stashed it into a pocket.

Unbuckling the belt from the man with two arrows in his chest, she sheathed his short sword in its scabbard and tossed it to Hywel. One man had been an archer, so she blended his quiver with hers, slung her bow over a shoulder, and reclaimed her javelin. Carys then trotted after her brother into the forest, the great trees dusted heavily with snow. They loped silently through the wood, away from the battle, like ghosts in the long shadows of the afternoon. Their footsteps crunched softly on the frozen ground, leaving little evidence of their passage. Sunlight filtered weakly through the dense underbrush.

The sounds of battle faded, and the eerie quiet unnerved her. It seemed all Cymru grieved the loss of her prince.

"Where are we headed, Hywel?" she asked, her voice pitched on a whisper. Though the English wore chain armor and lumbered about like oxen—easily heard in the silent forest—she didn't wish to draw attention in case scouts roamed this direction. Sound carried easily on the crisp winter air. Wearing dark green woolen leggings, leather jerkins, boots, and leather cowls covering their heads and shoulders, Carys and her brother blended in with the evergreen foliage and shadows.

"Our cousin, the prince, is dead," Hywel reminded her. "That means Cymru has fallen to the English. We've naught left of family, and nowhere to turn. I say we travel to the coast and find our way beyond Edward's reach."

The reminder of her husband Dafydd's death in battle only a few weeks past tore a fresh wound in Carys' aching heart. They'd been married only a few months, and her dreams of hearth, home, and children died along with him.

154

She considered her brother's words. She didn't know much of the world, but knew Longshank's reach stretched far. Was there such a place where his presence wasn't a blight upon the land?

Somehow, the English had crossed the Irfon river downstream today and attacked the Cymru army from behind. Hywel and Carys had been part of a small group of archers charged with holding the Orewin bridge, keeping the English on the south side of the river. Once the Marcher Lords attacked the Cymru flank, the English cavalry crossed the bridge unopposed. Equipped with better armor and weapons, the English had soon turned the battle into a slaughter. Carys and her brother were among the few who had survived. Their next steps would lead to their safety—or death.

* * *

Made in the USA
Las Vegas, NV
30 December 2024

15627909R00090